MAGIC & MURDER

STARRY HOLLOW WITCHES, BOOK 1

ANNABEL CHASE

RED PALM PRESS LLC

Magic & Murder

Starry Hollow Witches, Book 1

By Annabel Chase

Sign up for my newsletter here http://eepurl.com/ctYNzf and like me on Facebook so you can find out about new releases.

Cover Design by Alchemy

❀ Created with Vellum

CHAPTER 1

HILDA SANTIAGO WARNED me that women should always work in pairs. Hilda was a former repo agent herself, so she had the experience to pass along these pearls of wisdom. Of course, her pearls usually included a smattering of choice curse words and a long drag on her cigarette. Thankfully, I learned early on that wisdom came in many forms.

"Just because Alicia is out today doesn't mean I can't work," I said. "Logan has a stomach bug every other week." I never knew a kid could come down with so many illnesses. He was only six and he seemed prone to pick up any germ that came within a mile radius of him. My daughter was ten and I could count on one hand the number of school days she missed due to sickness. Then again, she was an aggressive hand washer.

"Fine," Hilda said, tossing the file across the metal desk. "Don't come crying to me when this guy verbally abuses you."

I flipped open the file. "I can handle verbal abuse. It's physical abuse I'm not too excited about." I scanned the paperwork. "Nice car. What happened?" Probably a divorce. That was often the outcome when money got divided. The

1

douchebag probably didn't want to give up his luxury sports car, but he needed to cry poverty in order to avoid paying half in the divorce settlement.

"Not sure. Just be careful," Hilda said. "I don't need to be down two agents."

"I'm a single mom with a mountain of bills," I said. "The only way I'm down and out is if someone puts me in the ground."

"Don't jinx yourself." Hilda stubbed out her cigarette and peered at me. "You're a good mom, Ember. You remind me of…"

I waved her off. "I know, I know. I remind you of your own mother. God bless her weary soul."

A hint of a smile appeared on her puckered lips. "Okay, so maybe I tell you that a little too often, but Rosario Santiago was as good as they come. They don't make women like her anymore."

"And the world is a sorrier place for it." Hilda could talk for another twenty minutes about her mother, depending on her mood.

"Good luck today," she said. "Try to come back in one piece."

"As long as I can get paid, I'll come back in as many pieces as necessary to walk through the door." I'd stopped answering my phone thanks to all of the collection agency calls I'd been receiving. I considered getting rid of the phone altogether, but I needed it for work and Marley's school, if nothing else.

I left the small, nondescript office building and sat in the tow truck while I studied the file. A cold Wawa coffee cup sat in the cup holder.

I looked up the address on my phone. The neighborhood was about twenty minutes away in a community called the Enclave. I could tell without looking that it was a gated community. That made things a little trickier, albeit not impossible. If I went now, then most of his neighbors had hopefully left for work already. I tried to spare people the embarrassment of public humiliation whenever possible. It was just good karma.

I switched on the radio as I traveled on back roads to the wealthy neighborhood. I had a weakness for 80's and 90's music, thanks to my father and his own musical obsession. My friends in high school thought I was strange for choosing Prince and Def Leppard over Taylor Swift and Justin Bieber, but some of my best memories were dancing with my dad to *Come on, Eileen.* He told me that my mother loved Madonna and Cyndi Lauper, so I made a point of knowing their songs inside and out in an effort to feel close to her. Although she died not long after I was born, my father made sure that he told me everything about her. My childhood bedtime included a chapter in a book and a story about my mother. My father never wanted me to feel deprived of her, even though we both knew that I had been.

The squat ranchers and broken-down bungalows began to morph into bigger and better houses. I was moving from the lower class neighborhoods to the middle class. Soon I'd reach the upper echelon of housing. While I waited at a traffic light, I took the opportunity to research the property taxes. I had a warped interest in how much someone paid each year for property taxes, especially in New Jersey, where the cost was notoriously high. Sure enough, this guy paid twenty-eight thousand dollars a year in property taxes. His house wasn't even particularly big, only 4500 square feet. This was the reason I lived in a two-bedroom apartment. Okay, it wasn't the whole reason. I also didn't have any money for a down payment on a mortgage. Minor details.

As I expected, the Enclave was a gated community. I hoped the person in the gatehouse was sympathetic to me.

Sometimes they looked the other way and didn't give the homeowner a heads-up that a repo agent was headed their way. It was best to do my job unhindered. I took one look at the older man behind the glass and knew I'd have my work cut out for me. He seemed like the kind of guy who wanted to befriend the owners in the neighborhood, particularly a Maserati-driving guy like James Litano.

I could tell by the scowl on his face that he didn't appreciate the presence of my tow truck on his turf. He pulled open the glass window as I rolled down mine. His bushy gray brow lifted when he saw my arm pumping and realized that my window was manual. No fancy electric for me.

"Are you lost?" the older man asked. "There's a Wal-Mart about three miles that way if that's what you're looking for."

"Wow," I exclaimed. "They let a Wal-Mart within three miles of this pristine community? What were the town planners thinking?" So maybe that response was not the way to win him over. Note to self: more teeth, less attitude.

His scowl deepened. "This is a private community. How can I help you?"

"I'm here to see James Litano," I said, producing my business card. He took it, examining it closely.

"Are you sure about this?" he asked, handing it back to me. I noticed that the scowl had been replaced by a look of concern.

"I have to do my job, just like you have to do yours," I said.

He leaned out of the window and peered into my truck. "You alone?"

Now he sounded like Hilda. What was it with older people and their concern for me?

"Yes, I'm alone. I assure you, though, I've done this job for two years now. I can handle Mr. Litano."

He hesitated briefly. "Do you carry?"

"No, I don't have a gun," I said. Although I'd considered it, statistically, it was more likely to be used on me, so I'd opted out. I had a ten-year-old daughter to consider. I did, however, keep a pocketknife close to hand. I wasn't a complete moron.

The gatekeeper glanced around nervously. "Listen, I'm going to let you through without calling up to the house. If anybody asks, you snuck in when a delivery van came through. Are we clear?"

I nodded vigorously.

He opened the gate and I continued into the development. Each house was grander than the last. Lawns were perfectly manicured, at least two acres per house. It was a far cry from my dumpy apartment complex. I bet these houses had laundry facilities on the second floor. I'd read about houses like that, magical places where you never had to carry a laundry basket up multiple flights of stairs. Maybe someday.

I finally arrived at my destination. 121 Arlington Street. I was disappointed by the street names in this development. I enjoyed the neighborhoods with a theme, like Robin Hood Lane and Maid Marian Court.

The Litano house was one of the largest houses on the block. While it was certainly big and grand, it was also tacky, with blinged-out lights and an animal throw rug on the covered front porch.

I fervently hoped there were no small children at home. I dreaded child witnesses more than verbal abuse. I hated the thought of scarring these children with the memory of their father's car being taken away. I also didn't like to speculate as to whether he took his frustration out on the children later.

I hopped out of the truck and set to work as quietly as possible. Although I could serve him with paperwork, I opted to get in and out quickly. The gatekeeper gave me the sense that knocking on the door was a bad idea. Maybe I'd get lucky and he'd still be asleep. After about ten minutes, I managed to get everything hooked up and climbed into the truck, ready to roll. The sound of the front door slamming alerted me to his presence.

Uh oh.

I heard a string of loud obscenities before I saw him in the side view mirror. He was a large man, about six feet three and solidly built, with thick, dark hair and olive skin. He wore sweatpants and an Eagles T-shirt. He'd probably been working out in his basement gym. He didn't come and tap on the window like I expected. Instead, he stood directly in front of the truck, a menacing look on his face. Smart.

"What in the hell do you think you're doing?" he shouted.

I wasn't stupid enough to roll down the window, so I yelled as loudly as I could. "What does it look like? I'm repossessing your car. You haven't made your payments. What did you expect to happen?"

"Release that car right now or you're going to regret it," he said. His deep, menacing voice rolled through the windshield like thunder.

"I'm afraid I can't do that, sir," I said. Maybe a little deference would break the tension.

"Listen up, you stupid bitch," he shouted.

Or maybe not.

I could see the throbbing vein in his neck. "Leave my car alone or I'm going to hurt you in ways you didn't know existed."

Well, that didn't sound promising.

I started the engine of the truck, which only served to aggravate him more. He began beating on the hood with his fists. I didn't want to run him over, but I was willing to hit the gas if he wasn't going to budge. I had to get out of here before he did serious damage to the vehicles or me.

"Last chance," he said.

From inside the safety of the truck, I shook my head. Then he did something that made my spine tingle with fear.

He smiled.

I watched as he reached into his pocket and pulled out a small object. Too small to be a gun. A phone? Was he going to call someone? That seemed more reasonable.

Then it hit me. It wasn't a phone. It was a lighter.

"Do you know what they call me?" he yelled.

I had a few ideas, but decided to keep them to myself in a futile attempt to live longer.

"Jimmy the Lighter."

First, he bent down and I watched in the mirror as he took the cap off the air valve. Sweet baby Elvis—he was letting the air out of the back tire. Then he began kicking the side of the vehicle with such force that the truck rocked back and forth. I realized that he was focused on damaging the gas tank.

I rolled the window down less than an inch. "Popcorn balls," I screamed. "Are you crazy?"

He laughed. "You're about to die and the best you got is popcorn balls? Lady, you gotta do better than that."

I was about to die. He'd just confirmed it.

"I have a daughter," I yelled. "I try to set a good example for her."

"Not anymore," he yelled back.

I watched in horror as a small flicker of light appeared and he tossed it toward the gas tank. The truck went up in flames almost immediately. My mind was in a blind panic. My only thought was of my daughter. Marley was only ten and I was about to leave her an orphan. We had no family except each other. Where would she go? Would she end up in foster care? Nobody adopted ten-year-olds these days. Not with IVF and surrogates and the ability to buy your own designer baby. My baby was gently used, Goodwill-style.

My heart seized.

My sweet darling with her midnight black hair and beautiful blue eyes. The new and improved mini-me. Everything I'd ever done since she was born was for her benefit. And now I was letting her down in the most spectacular way possible. Why had I insisted on coming here today? I should have just waited for Alicia and come tomorrow. I could have survived another day without cash.

Time slowed.

I felt the heat pressing upon me, sucking out the oxygen. The bright orange flames licked the metal frame of the vehicle. I watched it sweep across the hood. What was I doing? If I sat here, I would die. If I left the truck, I would die.

Out on the front lawn, Jimmy the Lighter laughed.

"Stop the fire. Stop the fire." My head was spinning. I knew I needed to stay calm and focus, but it wasn't happening.

He was going to kill me over a car. Deprive a child of her mother because of an object. A thing. What was wrong with this world?

Something snapped inside me. It felt like the pop and spark of a light bulb. A wave of energy rolled over me. My body began to tingle, especially my hands. I gripped the steering wheel.

"If only it would rain," I said aloud. That would take care of the fire.

The familiar sound of thunder caught my attention. When Jimmy glanced up at the sky, I knew I hadn't imagined it.

The downpour was swift and immediate. The rain fell so hard, it extinguished the flames in mere seconds. I couldn't believe my luck. I never had luck. I mean, I couldn't even win a dollar from a scratch-off lottery ticket.

Jimmy was soaking wet and very, very unhappy. He stared at me through the window like it was all my fault.

I didn't wait for his next move. I hit the gas and the truck lurched forward, nearly knocking him down in the process. Although the truck wasn't very fast with a flat tire, at least it moved.

"This isn't over," he screamed. "I'll find you—and your daughter."

I pressed the pedal as far as it would go and headed for the office, trying not to hyperventilate on the way. I had no clue what had happened back there and I couldn't bear to think about it. I had to have imagined the whole thing. Maybe this was all a bad dream. I'd ordered Chinese food last night. It was a distinct possibility.

Only when the gated community disappeared from my rear view did I allow myself to breathe.

It was a long drive back to the office.

CHAPTER 2

I KNOCKED on the door to apartment number twelve to pick up my daughter. Miss Kowalski had lived in the building for over twenty years and was a lovely but lonely old lady. I remembered the way her eyes had lit up when Marley and I first moved into the building. She'd been so thrilled to have a child around, even if she wasn't her own. Miss Kowalski was the epitome of your friendly neighborhood cat lady. From our conversations about her personal life, I got the distinct impression that her life had been a string of failed relationships and a single, heart-wrenching miscarriage from which she never fully recovered. I was only too happy to let her watch Marley after school so that I could work. From my point of view, she was a godsend.

The door jerked open and I stared into the face of my mini-me. She still had the chubby cheeks of childhood, but a pair of blue eyes that looked as though they'd seen everything and then some. Her teachers called her Matilda, after the gifted child from the Roald Dahl book. Marley fascinated them with her abilities. She also happened to be an anxious child, constantly worrying about outcomes and consequences. The school counselor had assured me that it was a result of her intelligence. Marley often lived deep inside her own head and I had to make an effort to drag her out of there on occasion.

"What happened to you?" Marley asked. Her tone was a mixture of concern and accusation. She didn't care for my job because she'd read several articles on the Internet about when repo jobs went sideways. Parental controls only did so much.

"Nothing," I replied, breezing past her into the apartment. "Good afternoon, Miss Kowalski. How's my Marley today?"

"Ask her yourself," Miss Kowalski said. "She doesn't need an adult to speak for her. Go on, Marley. Tell her about Fanta."

Miss Kowalski had three cats: Fanta, Minx, and Trixie.

"Fanta let me pet her without biting me today," Marley said proudly. Fanta was a known biter, so this was big news.

"Congratulations," I said. "I wonder what you did to deserve such royal treatment."

"I told her it was only a matter of time before Fanta warmed to her," Miss Kowalski said. Sure, it only took four years. No time at all.

"Did you do your homework?" I asked. I don't know why I bothered to ask. Marley always did her homework the second she came home. As much as I tried to parent her, she was already doing a decent job without me.

Marley nodded vigorously. "There were several grammatical mistakes in the homework," she said. "Do you think I should tell Mr. Jacobs tomorrow?"

This was a frequent discussion in our home. We weren't sure of the etiquette. Did Mr. Jacobs want to be corrected by a ten-year-old? We weren't sure. Most of the time, we kept the information to ourselves, unless it was particularly egregious.

"Let's sleep on it," I said. "Thanks, Miss Kowalski. We'll see you tomorrow."

Miss Kowalski gave me a wave from the couch, her gaze fixed on the television where some Americans were trying to prove they had talent.

"Anytime," she said vaguely.

Marley and I made our way upstairs to our apartment. Our Yorkie, Prescott Peabody III, barely looked up from the sofa when we entered.

"I assume he got walked today," I said.

"Of course," Marley said, rushing to the sofa to pet the dog. "We had him out an hour ago. I wish he got along better with the cats, so that he could stay in the apartment with us after school. He must get lonely by himself."

"We tried that already, remember?" And it was an unmitigated disaster. We were lucky that all four animals got out alive.

"He misses us when we're not here," she said.

"I'm sure he does, but there isn't really a choice in the matter."

I went into the kitchen to see what was available for dinner. I wasn't much of a planner, so I was always scrambling at the last minute to pull together ingredients for a quick meal. I felt guilty about it, but at least I wasn't raising her on a diet of fast food. Small favors.

"What's for dinner?" Marley asked. "Can I help you make it?"

Marley was always offering to help me. To the untrained eye, it appeared as though she was a keen helper, but I knew better. The reality was that Marley just liked to be by my side as much as possible. If that meant standing hip to hip in the kitchen making dinner, then so be it. She even slept with me at night, even though we lived in a two-bedroom apartment. I had deliberately chosen two bedrooms, even though the rent was higher, because I wanted Marley to grow up in her own space. It turned out that she didn't want her own space. She wanted to be wrapped around my leg at all times. The sleeping arrangements weren't too bad, to be honest. It wasn't like I had a boyfriend. Marley slept like the hands of the clock, though. I was awakened at various points each night by a hand in my face or a knee in my groin. I usually had to get up out of bed and drag her to the other side until she wormed her way back across the great divide in her sleep. Miss Kowalski told me I wasn't doing her any favors by indulging her need for comfort, but Marley had lost her father four years ago, and I knew that she suffered from anxiety about losing me as well. If there was anything I could do to quell her stress, then I was willing to do it.

"How about spaghetti Bolognese?" I asked.

"But you hate the way I eat spaghetti," Marley protested.

It was true. Marley did not have a knack for eating spaghetti on a fork. The thin strands of pasta constantly slid through the gaps in the fork and, no matter how many times I showed Marley how to wrap it, she simply couldn't master the skill. On the one hand, it was nice to see her fail. Things always came so easily to her. I felt that it was character-building that she had to work harder to achieve this.

"I'll make an exception," I said.

She cast a suspicious look at me. "Why?"

I struggled for a response. Because a maniac tried to kill me and leave you an orphan? No, I couldn't tell Marley the truth. Hilda and I had agreed that Jimmy wouldn't be able to trace me back here. There was no reason to act like anything was wrong. Marley already suffered separation anxiety. I wasn't about to make it worse.

"Because you got an A on your math quiz," I finally said.

"How did you know?" she asked. "I hadn't told you yet."

I tousled her hair. "Because you always get A's on your quizzes. Why should today be any different?"

"Sounds good to me," Marley said. "Do we have any garlic bread?"

"I'll check the freezer." A quick peek revealed no garlic bread. "Sorry, honey. Maybe next time." To her credit, she was unfazed.

"Can I have chocolate milk tonight?"

"Sure." I tried not to sweat the small stuff. An occasional chocolate milk wasn't going to kill her. She was skinny as a rail with relatively good eating habits. She ate broccoli like it was the last stalk on earth. It took me into adulthood to like broccoli. She was already light years ahead of me—in so many ways.

"Can you feed the dog while I get started on this?" I asked.

Marley rushed to complete the task. She was more goal-oriented than any ten-year-old had a right to be. Then again, I hoped that it saved her from a life like mine. If Marley grew up to be a repo agent, I will definitely have failed as a parent.

I filled a pot with water and turned on the stove while Marley fed the dog. This was my favorite part of the day, where Marley shared all the gossip from school. I knew which kids were troublemakers and which kids were being bullied. Because Marley was the polar opposite of me—quiet and well behaved—she was able to observe others without anyone noticing her. Occasionally, she would report her findings to the teacher if she felt that it was a serious matter, but mostly she liked to report to me.

Over dinner, she asked me about my day. Sometimes I gave her the details, but today was not one of those days.

"It was a very cool car," I said. "A Maserati."

She whistled. "Fancy. Was it a divorce?"

"Don't think so." Just a mobster who was feeling entitled.

"Did he yell at you?"

"A little bit." Or a lot.

"I'm sorry," Marley said, and my heart nearly split in two.

"Sweetheart, you don't have to be sorry. You didn't do anything."

"But if you didn't have to take care of me, then you wouldn't need to take these horrible jobs. You could get your degree and get a better job."

I set down my fork and stared at her. "Marley Rose, I don't ever want to hear talk like that again. Do you understand? You are worth all the degrees in existence. I would sacrifice anything to take care of you. In fact, forget I said that. It's not even a sacrifice. It's an honor. Got it?"

Marley blinked her big blue eyes. She understood.

"This is good chocolate milk," she said. "Did you put an extra squirt in it?"

I shrugged. "I may have. A good chef never reveals her secrets."

"I think that's a magician," Marley said.

"Know-it-all."

After dinner, I cleaned up the kitchen while Marley showered. She preferred that I stand outside the bathroom door while she showered in case she fell and got hurt, but I'd been working on getting her out of the habit. I didn't want her to worry about routine tasks. Sleeping and showering should not involve a ten-year-old's mother. Although I knew this on an intellectual level, when she leveled that sweet, desperate gaze at me, it was tough to resist.

I changed into pajamas and snuggled beside her in bed for reading time. It was part of our bedtime ritual. Ever since she was old enough to read on her own, we read side by side until it was time for lights out. A Kindle was a blessing for me because I could continue to read with the lit screen while Marley went to sleep.

I noticed a different book cover in her hands. "You finished the last book already?"

She nodded. "I finished at school today during lunch."

"The library is going to run out of books for you," I said.

"That's why digital books are so great."

PP3 began to bark and shot off the bed like a hairy bullet. I chased after him, calling his name.

"No bark," I said firmly. "Mr. Peterson will be down here in a heartbeat to complain."

The dog ignored me, standing in front of the apartment door and barking loudly. A pounding of fists on the other side of the door made me jump.

"I hear you in there, Ember Rose. Why don't you open the door and let me in, you little pig?"

My heart lodged in my throat at the sound of his voice.

"Not by the hair of my chin-chin-chin," I replied, with as much bravado as I could manage. I ran to the counter and unplugged my cell phone. "I'm calling the police right now."

"Mom?" Marley called from the bedroom. "Who are you talking to?"

"Stay in your room," I commanded.

Prescott Peabody III continued to run back and forth in front of the door, barking like the attack dog he wasn't.

"I'll huff and I'll puff," Jimmy said through the door. "On second thought, it might be easier if you huff and puff."

What did that mean? "Sorry, Jimmy. I'm not a smoker. As it happens, I'm in pretty decent shape."

Marley appeared in the doorway of her bedroom. "What's going on?"

I whipped toward her. "I said go to your room and lock the door."

She shook her head, an expression of pure terror on her face. "Not without you and PP3."

What had I done? I'd brought this criminal element to our home to threaten us. If I lived until tomorrow, I promised myself I'd get another job.

I dialed the number for emergency services.

"9-1-1. What's your emergency?"

I didn't get to answer. The door came flying off the hinges and nearly struck me. I ran into the kitchen and grabbed the nearest knife. Unfortunately for me, it was a butter knife.

"Nice hovel you got here," Jimmy said, surveying the room.

The dog lunged at him, growling and biting his pant leg. Jimmy laughed and shook him off with minimal effort.

"PP3, come," Marley called from the bedroom. To my relief, the dog obeyed.

"I've called the police," I said, and wielded the butter knife like a saber.

"You called, but you didn't finish," he said. "I have ears, you know." He pulled a small silver item from his pocket. "And a lighter, as it happens." He bit his bottom lip, pretending to think. "How long until the fire trucks get here, do you think? Would the whole building burn or just your place?"

He flicked the lid open and smiled.

"The other people in this building are innocent," I said. "My daughter is innocent. Hell, my dog is innocent."

"No one is innocent," he said. "Not in the world we live in."

A tiny flame appeared and he tossed the lighter onto the shaggy green carpet.

"You don't have to do this," I said.

"I know I don't have to," he replied, "but it's fun." He winked. "Have fun huffing and puffing, little pig."

I started to run toward the bedrooms, but he was too fast. He grabbed my leg and I stumbled to the floor. I inhaled the smoke wafting from the burning carpet and began to cough.

"You need to go or you're going to burn, too," I said. Not that I minded.

"You forget I have experience with this," he replied. "I know how much time I have." His nails pierced my skin and I screamed.

"Release her," a voice commanded.

The police were here? But how?

"Make me," Jimmy said gruffly.

An unseen hand sent him flying through the air and he slammed into the sofa, tipping it backward. The flames had multiplied since my last glance and I realized that I was sweating.

"*Famem*," another voice said, and the flames disappeared as quickly as they'd developed.

Three strangers stood in my shoebox apartment—two women and a man—each taller and more beautiful than the next. With their white-blond hair and pale skin, they reminded me of Targaryens from *Game of Thrones*.

On the other side of the room, Jimmy groaned and managed to get back on his feet.

"Is this person threatening to harm you?" the man asked.

"Gee, what gave you that impression?" I replied.

Jimmy stared at the trio. "Which one of you threw me across the room?" His eyes narrowed at the sight of the man. "It must've been you."

"Well, that's rather sexist of you," the female on the left said. "Actually, it was me."

"Nice try, sweetie." Jimmy reached for the lighter in his pocket.

"I don't think so," the other female said, and snapped her fingers. The lighter broke into pieces and fell onto the floor.

"What the hell?" Jimmy stared at his hand, trying to grasp what just happened.

"Who are you?" I asked. Aliens were the answer that sprang to mind. They were aliens who'd come to collect their earthly human specimens.

"All in good time," the man said. "First, we must deal with the problem." He waved a hand in the shape of an 's' and Jimmy froze in place.

The taller of the two women approached him and pressed her hands against the side of his head. "*Obliviscatur.*"

She released his head and he blinked. "Where am I?"

"You went out for a pack of cigarettes," the woman said.

"I went out for a pack of cigarettes," he repeated.

"And you were never here," she added.

"I was never here." He crossed the room and exited via the broken door. Once he left, the shorter woman waved a hand and the door snapped back into place as though nothing had happened.

"How are you doing that?" I asked in disbelief.

"Simple," the woman said. "I'm a witch."

CHAPTER 3

"I'm sorry," I said. "Did you just say you're a witch?"

She swept her white-blond hair out of her eyes. "That is correct."

"Mom, who are these people?" Marley stood a safe distance away, holding PP3 tightly.

"Yarrow, you need to come with us," the male Targaryen said to me.

"I don't know what a Yarrow is, but my name is Ember and I'm not going anywhere with you."

The trio exchanged confused glances.

"You are Yarrow Rose," the man said. "Daughter of Lily Hawthorne-Rose and Nathaniel Rose."

Now it was my turn to be confused. "Those were my parents, but like I said, my name is Ember."

"And who is this?" the older female asked, pointing to Marley. "A half-sister, perhaps?"

"She wishes," Marley exclaimed. Oh, my daughter thought that was just hilarious. If I lived through this night, I would never live it down.

"This is my daughter," I said. I wasn't about to tell them

her name. "Thank you ever so much for taking care of the pyromaniac killer in my apartment, but who are you and why are you here?"

"My name is Aster Rose-Muldoon," the younger blonde said. "This is my sister, Linnea, and my brother, Florian."

"Rose?" I echoed. "You're related to my father?"

"Our mother, Hyacinth, is your father's sister," Aster said.

I'd never heard of an Aunt Hyacinth. Then again, my father never spoke of any family apart from my mother. It never occurred to me that he was hiding something.

"So why are you here now? I'm twenty-eight years old and I've never heard of any of you."

"Your father kept you shrouded in secrecy," Linnea said. "He didn't want us to find you."

"Well, my father was a smart man," I said. "If he didn't want you to find me, then he must've had a pretty good reason."

"Petty squabbles," Linnea said. "Water under the troll's bridge."

I thought about everything I'd just witnessed. "So can you all do magic?"

Aster nodded. "And so can you. You're a witch, Ember. As was your mother."

"And your father was a wizard," Florian added. "Like me."

I stared at them, my mouth hanging open. "If you were an enormous Scottish guy called Hagrid, this moment might be more believable."

"You used magic earlier today, didn't you?" Linnea asked. "That's how we were able to pinpoint your location."

"We believe your father used a suppression spell to keep your magic from manifesting and a cloaking spell to shield you from those of us in Starry Hollow who wished to find you," Aster added.

"That was magic?" I whispered. It had certainly seemed like magic at the time, but how?

"We come into our magic around age eleven," Aster said. "Your father likely performed a spell that kept your abilities under wraps. He knew that if you used magic, then we'd be able to track you."

"Mom, I'm going to be eleven next year," Marley whispered. "Will I have magic, too?"

Aster smiled at her. "There's a good chance you will, young one. I have two children. Little boys. They will be so excited to meet you."

I wrapped my arms protectively around Marley. "I don't know about a family reunion. I appreciate you saving us, but I have to trust my father's instincts. If he didn't want you to find us, then he had a reason."

"He did," Linnea said. "But it's not what you might think. Come with us and our mother will explain all."

"It isn't safe here for you any longer," Florian said. "That man is a mobster, isn't he? I've seen enough movies with the human mafia. We erased his memory of this evening's events, but not of you entirely. I doubt he will rest until he exacts his revenge."

"If you stay here, you're both as good as dead," Linnea said.

Marley clung to me, and I felt her small fingers dig into my back. "We should go with them, Mom."

I kissed the side of her head. "Where would we go?" I asked.

"The town is called Starry Hollow. It's on the coast of North Carolina." Aster fixed her attention on Marley. "There are lovely schools and lots of magical children to play with. You will both be very happy there, I promise."

"No one can promise happiness," I said.

Aster bit her lip. "Happier than you are here? Will that do?"

I didn't know what to do. Three strangers with crazy powers were standing in my apartment telling me that my life was in danger and that I was a witch. Despite the insanity of the moment, the voice inside me urged me to listen. I had to trust that voice. It was one that had saved my life on many occasions.

"Do you have any money?" I asked. "I don't want to stiff my landlord for the rest of the lease. He's an old man and it's his only source of income."

Florian frowned. "Money is not a problem." He snapped his fingers and a check appeared in his hand. "Say the amount and it will appear here."

"But will the money appear in my bank account?" That seemed to be the pertinent issue.

Florian nodded. "You can trust us, Ember. We're your family."

"Trust is earned," I said firmly. "Family or not."

Linnea broke into a broad smile that brightened her beautiful face. The Rose-Muldoons certainly seemed to get the lion's share of the attractive genes. "You will not regret this choice, Yarrow Rose."

I pressed my fingers to my temples. "Listen. I go on two conditions. One is that you stop calling me Yarrow. My name is Ember. Two is that my dog comes, too. He's nine and we can't leave him behind."

Three white-blond heads turned toward the dog sitting in the doorway. I had to admit that he looked pathetic with his overgrown brown hair and deep, sad eyes. But Prescott Peabody III was ours and I refused to leave him.

"I am sure your new home can accommodate a small dog," Aster said. She extended her hand. "Come now, before the man returns."

"How do we get there?" I asked. "Do we fly on broomsticks or something?" I couldn't believe the words coming out of my mouth. Did I seriously just ask about riding on a broomstick?

"We use magic," Florian said. "Like a magical wormhole. The spell transports us from one place to another."

"A magical wormhole," I repeated.

"That sounds cool," Marley said. For once, she didn't sound scared.

I glanced down at my fuzzy pajamas. "What about our clothes? Our belongings?"

"We can take anything that you can't live without," Linnea said. She surveyed the nondescript bedroom. "But I suspect there aren't too many items that fall under that description."

She was right. There really weren't.

"Join hands," Linnea instructed. "As long as you keep hold of the dog inside the circle, he will be transported with us."

I linked my arm through Marley's and we all joined hands as my three cousins began to chant. I didn't understand a word of what they were saying, but I felt the energy around us change. The air began to feel heavy and crackled around us. Without warning, I felt like I was falling. Then I was weightless and everything around me turned to inky darkness.

When the darkness finally receded, I found myself standing on a footbridge overlooking a river. The cousins stood in front of me and Marley was beside me, clutching the dog and looking green around the gills.

"Are you okay?" I asked.

She nodded her pale and sweaty head but didn't speak.

I looked around. "Where are we?"

"We have to stop at the border and show ID before we can enter the town," Florian said. "Standard procedure."

"Border patrol," I repeated. "But we don't have passports. You said we were going someplace in North Carolina!"

"Calm yourself, Yarrow...I mean, Ember," Linnea said in her soothing tone. "We haven't left the United States. Starry Hollow regulates its borders. For one thing, we need to keep unsuspecting humans from entering."

"How many humans end up at the border on a daily basis?" I queried.

"Not many. It's the paranormal tourists that keep border patrol busy," Aster said. "Thanks to its location, Starry Hollow is a premiere destination. My sister owns a busy inn that caters to the trade."

"Can't you use magic to hide the town from Muggles?" Marley asked.

"What's a Muggle?" Florian queried.

"A non-magic person. It's a Harry Potter reference," I explained. "Marley's a big fan."

"Yes, I suppose she's right then," Florian said. "We do use magic to keep the town veiled from humans, but we get the occasional drunk or magic seeker who wanders too close to the border."

"We don't have ID," I said. "How will we get in?"

"Mother sent word to the border agents," Linnea said. "It won't be a problem."

"And they'll just take her word for it?" I asked.

The three cousins laughed.

"Oh, yes," Florian said. "You'll understand when you meet her."

I suddenly felt ill at ease. Aunt Hyacinth sounded like a big deal in Starry Hollow. "Will I meet her tonight?"

"At supper. She's hosting at seven," Linnea said.

"But it's already nine," I said.

"Not anymore," Florian said. "Magical wormholes sometimes set you back an hour or two."

Could it set me back a lifetime so I could start over?

Linnea looked me up and down. "You'll need suitable attire."

I glanced down at my pajamas. "What? Fluffy bunny slippers won't cut the mustard?"

The cousins exchanged uneasy glances.

"Mother is..." Florian heaved a sigh. "A force to be reckoned with. She will expect you to look a certain way."

"And talk a certain way," Aster added.

I narrowed my eyes. "I can't help my Jersey accent. It's where I'm from."

"Yes, that's unfortunate," Aster said. "While we can't tackle the accent, we can tackle the clothes. And I know just the place."

Linnea rolled her eyes. "Don't you dream of taking her to Milly Howlitzer. It's perfectly clear that's not her style."

"It could become her style," Aster said. "Pink and green is a lovely color combination with her complexion."

I waved my hands in front of my face. "No, no. Sorry. I don't do pink."

"Me neither," Marley said, folding her arms.

"Very well then," Aster said. "I'll whisk her over to Shining Stars then."

Linnea's nose wrinkled. "I didn't say dress her like a prostitute. What about The Pointy Hat?"

"Perfect," Aster agreed. "They have a tween section there as well."

Marley brightened. "I get an outfit, too?"

"Of course," Aster said. "Mother will expect both of you to be presentable."

Florian handled the female border agent with his boyish charm. By the time we passed through, she was tripping over herself to get his number. Not that it was a surprise. They were ridiculously attractive siblings. I felt like a wet wash-cloth standing next to them. I hoped not everyone in Starry Hollow was as good-looking. I'd be forever known as 'New Jersey pretty.'

A black car pulled up and the doors popped open.

"Oh, good," Linnea said. "Mother sent her driver."

Wow. Aunt Hyacinth had a driver?

"We'll take the car to The Pointy Hat," Aster said.

The driver's side window rolled down and a man poked out his head. "I'm afraid your mother insists on no detours. She's anxious to meet her niece."

Aster muttered under her breath. "Fine, I'll have to use magic."

"Is it a problem to use magic?" I asked. I didn't want to cause trouble the moment we stepped over the town border.

"No, no trouble," Aster replied. "Just not as much fun."

"Not from where I'm sitting," Marley said, her blue eyes shining.

"A simple shift dress," Linnea said. "And a floral dress for the girl."

Aster studied us a moment before waving her hand and saying, "*Vestio.*"

I glanced down at my clothes. My pajamas were replaced with a tasteful navy blue dress and a pair of pumps. A string of pearls rested around my neck.

"Pearls, Aster?" Linnea queried.

"You know how much Mother likes them," Aster said. "I'm just trying to give Ember her best chance at a first impression."

"I love my dress," Marley said, fluffing her floral skirt. "I've never owned a dress before."

"You did once," I said. "You just don't remember." I

remembered it all too well. How could I forget the dress she wore to her father's funeral?

Prescott Peabody III yelped at our feet. I scooped him up and he licked my cheek.

"Yes, it's still us, buddy," I said. "Don't worry."

"Let's go," Linnea said, jerking her head toward the car. "Mother doesn't like to be kept waiting."

CHAPTER 4

"WELCOME TO THORNHOLD," Florian said, as the car pulled into a semi-circular driveway.

The house was...not a house. It was a sprawling manor straight out of a Jane Austen novel.

"How do you not get lost in there?" Marley asked, her eyes popping.

"We grew up in this house," Aster said. "We know all of its nooks and crannies."

We stepped out of the car and followed the trio up the sweeping staircase to the oversized front doors. A butler was ready and waiting in the foyer. He was bald and wore an unbecoming pair of glasses that only served to make his head appear rounder.

"Welcome home, Master Florian," he said. "Miss Aster and Miss Linnea."

"Good evening, Simon," Linnea said. "This is our cousin, Ember, and her daughter, Marley."

"And Prescott Peabody III," Marley added, holding up the dog.

Simon gave us a friendly smile and patted the Yorkie's head. "It will be nice to have a dog around for a change."

"Now, Simon," Aster said. "Mind yourself."

"I've been instructed to escort you to the dining room," Simon said.

"Very good then," Florian said.

The dining room was the size of my entire apartment. A huge oval table sat in the middle of the room with a chandelier directly above it. At first glance, it appeared to be made of crystal, but the flashes of colorful light emanating from it suggested magic was at work.

Hyacinth Rose-Muldoon swept into the room wearing a hot pink kaftan. Her white-blond hair was pulled back in an elegant chignon and she wore a pair of tiny kitten heels that matched her frock. At first, I thought the design on the kaftan was floral, but upon closer inspection, I realized that it was decorated with faces. Fluffy, white faces, every single one the same. I was rendered speechless, which happened almost...never.

Marley pinched my hip. "Mom, she's covered in cats. She's the ultimate cat lady."

I quickly shushed her and prayed that Aunt Hyacinth didn't overhear her. I didn't know what kind of witchy powers she had. The last thing I needed was to raise a toad instead of a child. I wasn't overly fond of amphibians.

"Now this is a momentous occasion," Aunt Hyacinth said, crossing the room to greet us. She cupped my chin in her hands and studied my face intently. "Well, you inherited your father's nose. That's a shame. Your mother's coloring is also a loss. No one will believe you're a Rose without proof."

"Proof?" I queried. "Like a DNA test?"

Aunt Hyacinth tittered. "Yes, why not? Like a DNA test." She moved on to inspect Marley. "A pleasure to meet you, young lady. We were not even aware of your existence. A shame that you're only half a witch, but we shall take what we can get." She gripped Marley by the chin and jerked her head from side to side, like she was inspecting a mare. I expected her to check Marley's teeth and gums, too.

"You're squeezing my face," Marley said, through gritted teeth.

"Good bones, despite the unfortunate taint of human genes," Aunt Hyacinth said. "How old are you?"

"Ten," Marley replied.

"Too young for the Black Cloak Academy," Aunt Hyacinth said. "She'll enroll in the middle school for now. Hopefully, she'll come into her magic within the next year, and then we'll see her transferred to the academy. All Roses attend the academy. It's tradition."

A longhaired, white cat trotted in behind Aunt Hyacinth and sat at her feet, staring at us with bright blue eyes. She was a gorgeous cat and she seemed to know it.

"Is that the same cat as the one on your dress?" I asked, inclining my head.

"Who else would adorn my clothing except my Precious?" Aunt Hyacinth said, scooping up the cat in her arms.

I laughed. "I wouldn't have pegged you for a *Lord of the Rings* fan."

Aunt Hyacinth's expression shriveled in a way that Marley and I called 'stinky sock face.'

"I don't know what you mean."

"Oh, her name is actually Precious?" I said, blinking. "I thought for sure her name was going to be Crystal or China." The cat was so beautifully delicate.

Aunt Hyacinth gave me a look that would have withered an oak tree. "She's not a stripper, for Nature's sake. She's my familiar."

Linnea step forward to intervene. "You'll have to excuse her, Mother. She knows nothing of Starry Hollow or witches, for that matter. She'll have to learn everything from the ground up."

Aunt Hyacinth appraised me coolly. "Yes, in some ways that might be a benefit. Her bad habits won't be magical. Therefore, they will be easier to break."

"What bad habits?" I asked. I didn't bite my nails or leave the lid off the toothpaste. Okay, I had a major sweet tooth, but I didn't think that qualified as a bad habit. Just a bad diet.

Aunt Hyacinth snapped her fingers and a tiny silver bell appeared in her hand. Although she rang it, I heard no sound.

"Why don't we sit for supper?" Aunt Hyacinth said. "Food will be served in just a moment."

The bell disappeared as quickly as it had materialized. Aunt Hyacinth took her place at the head of the table and gestured to the two seats adjacent to her. "Yarrow, you will sit to my left. Marley, you will sit to my right."

Marley shot me a baleful look before taking her seat across from me. I knew she would have preferred to sit beside me. The table was so wide that, even though she sat across from me, she seemed a mile away.

"My name is Ember," I said.

Aunt Hyacinth gave me a blank look. "That's absurd. Who would name a child Ember?"

Because Yarrow was so popular? "My name has been Ember for as long as I can remember," I said. "My father must've changed it."

Aunt Hyacinth sniffed. "I see. Well, I suppose it will have to do." Her expression brightened. "First, a toast to our new additions," she said, raising her flute of what appeared to be champagne.

I lifted the flute to my nose and listened to the soothing sound of fizz. I'd never tasted champagne before.

"*Carpe noctem*," Hyacinth said.

Everyone else raised their glasses and repeated the phrase.

"What's the saying here?" I asked, after I'd taken my first sip of champagne. It was more tart than I was expecting.

"*Carpe noctem,*" Florian repeated.

"*Carpe diem* means seize the day in Latin," Marley said. "So *carpe noctem* must mean seize the night."

Aunt Hyacinth gave her an approving nod. "Well done, young lady. Are you studying Latin in school?"

Marley snorted. "Not exactly. There's this movie my babysitter let me watch called *Dead Poet's Society*. *Carpe diem* is the theme of the story."

"The theme?" Aunt Hyacinth repeated, clearly impressed.

"Why do you say this before meals?" I asked.

"It's our family motto," Aster replied. "It's also on the family crest you see over the fireplace." She pointed above the mantel where an enormous banner adorned the wall. It had a dark blue background and featured a full moon and stars with a red rose in front of the moon. *Carpe noctem* was embroidered along the bottom.

"It's so cool," Marley said. "So that's my family crest, too?"

"Apparently," I said.

At that moment, several silver trays floated out of the neighboring room, presumably the kitchen, and came to rest on the table. It gave free-range food a whole new meaning. Once all of the silver serving platters were on the table, Aunt Hyacinth snapped her fingers again and the lids popped off. The smells alone were intoxicating. I've never been what you would call a foodie. My idea of a fancy meal is the top sirloin at Applebee's, but for some reason, I could smell every herb and spice in the dishes. It was both overwhelming and incredible.

"Mom, are you okay?" Marley called from across the table.

My head snapped to attention. "What? Why?"

"Your eyes are watering," Marley said. "I thought you might be crying."

"No, of course not," I said, using my cloth napkin to wipe away the tears. "It's all of these amazing spices." I felt bad that Marley thought I was upset. It was a very rare occasion for her to see me cry. In fact, the last time would have been four years ago when her father died. My own father didn't raise any crybabies.

"I imagine your mother is adjusting to her new experience," Aunt Hyacinth said. "The door has been unlocked and now her inner magic is pushing it wide open."

"Why is this happening now?" I asked. "I've been in plenty of stressful situations in my life. None of them resulted in a release of magic."

Aunt Hyacinth ignored my question. "What would you like to eat? Roast chicken? It has lemon and salt and some other lovely spices that I won't divulge. Secret recipe, you see."

"It all looks delicious," I said. "I'll try a little of everything." I glanced quickly at Marley. She was not what you would call an adventurous eater. If it wasn't breaded or wrapped in a hotdog bun, she was disinclined to eat it. "Marley, why don't you try a few pieces of chicken?" I hoped she wouldn't embarrass me in front of our newfound family.

Marley wrinkled her nose in disgust. "It has the skin on."

"The skin is the best part," Florian said, ripping off a layer of skin and popping the crunchy bit into his mouth.

"Then you can have my portion," Marley said. "Because I'm not eating any of it."

"Marley," I snapped. "Remember your manners."

Marley looked at me scornfully. "What manners? We're from New Jersey."

I tried in vain to kick her under the table, but my foot wouldn't reach. I found myself sliding off the base of the chair in an effort to reach her. It wasn't until I actually slid onto the floor that I realized I was making a complete fool of myself. So magic didn't cure that personality trait then.

"Ember, are you quite all right?" Aster asked. She was unfortunate enough to be seated next to me.

I climbed back onto my chair and smoothed my hair back. "Sorry about that. I got a cramp in my leg."

I glanced back at Marley to see her with a full plate of food, eating without complaint. My brow lifted.

"Sometimes children just need a little encouragement," Aunt Hyacinth said simply.

I frowned. "Did you use magic?"

"Perhaps a very gentle sort," Aunt Hyacinth said softly.

"Can you teach me?" I was suddenly beginning to see another benefit to learning magic.

"I won't teach you myself, but I will certainly arrange for people who can," Aunt Hyacinth said. "It's important to sharpen your skills."

"So tell me about my father. Are you his younger sister?"

Aunt Hyacinth reached over and patted my hand. "Well, aren't you sweet? No, I am, in fact, your father's older sister. He was always a difficult one. Wanting to do things his own way. No one was surprised when he fell in love with your mother. She was as different as they come in the Starry Hollow community."

Everything I knew about my mother came from my father. It seemed surreal to be sitting with people who knew her for most of her life.

"What was so different about her? She was a witch like the rest of you, right?"

Aunt Hyacinth took a dainty sip from her flute. "Yes, she was a witch, but she didn't care much about magic. She didn't want to stay in Starry Hollow. She was a wayfarer at heart, and my brother was only too happy to indulge her. They planned to move away after you were born, but, sadly, your mother died before that happened."

"So is that why my father left?" I asked. "Because she would have wanted him to?"

"Partly," Aunt Hyacinth said. "He was also angry that no one here could save her. He turned his back on us because he felt that we'd turned our backs on him."

"Is that true?" Marley asked. "Could magic have saved her?"

Aunt Hyacinth lowered her head. "Certainly not, child. Magic cannot reverse death in any meaningful way. Your father could not see past his grief to see sense. He snuck off in the middle of the night with young Yarrow and never looked back."

"What happened to me?" I asked. "Where has my magic been all these years?" I could think of so many times that a little magic would've come in handy in my life. There were the trivial times like when Kelly Foster tried to bully me on the bus in eighth grade, but there were also the more serious times like the death of my husband, Karl. Maybe if I'd had magic, he never even would've been a truck driver. He never would've been on the highway in the middle of the night and fallen asleep. So many what ifs. My head was spinning.

"From what we can gather, your father performed a spell on you that suppressed your magic before you turned eleven," my aunt explained. "He'd also cast a cloaking spell, so that no one here could track your location or his."

"Why didn't the spells break after he died?" I asked.

"Magic doesn't work that way," Linnea said. "The spell likely weakened, which is why when you had a moment of extreme stress, the magic was unleashed like a snake that had been coiled too long."

"Yes," Aunt Hyacinth agreed. "I believe that my brother's death weakened his cloaking spell and your near-death experience triggered your magic. It was a house of cards that came tumbling down all at once."

"And so what happened?" I asked. "Suddenly you got the bat signal in the sky that showed a map of New Jersey?"

"Cool," Florian said. "Are you a *Batman* fan? I prefer the darker stuff, not that Tim Burton monstrosity."

Aunt Hyacinth gently tapped her fork on the side of her flute. "Florian, stay focused on the subject at hand, please."

Florian's head drooped. He seemed accustomed to such reprimands.

"Mom won't let me watch the *Batman* movies," Marley said. "She says they're too violent."

Florian gave her a wink. "That's what older cousins are for."

I chose to ignore his comment. There seemed to be bigger fish to fry at the moment than whether my ten-year-old watched PG-13 movies.

"So why bring us here now?" I asked. "Marley and I have a life in New Jersey. What's the matter of urgency that brings us to Starry Hollow?"

Aunt Hyacinth appeared miffed by the question. "Why, you are a Rose, of course. You belong in Starry Hollow. I can't imagine that your life in New Jersey was very hospitable. My children said it was like extracting you from a war zone."

My cheeks reddened. "It was an apartment building in Maple Shade. It was hardly a war zone." I mean, it wasn't Newark.

"A man tried to kill you," Linnea said. "It isn't safe for you there anymore."

She had a point. Jimmy the Lighter was a member of the mob. He wasn't going to just give up and fuggedaboutit. He would pursue me until he exacted his revenge. I glanced across the table at Marley, who was busily gnawing on a chicken leg. I had to protect her at all costs.

"Where will we live here? I need a job. I don't have any money. I couldn't even afford to buy the clothes I'm wearing tonight."

"I will gladly help you get started here," Aunt Hyacinth said. "We are family, after all. Family sticks together. It was a sentiment your father never learned, unfortunately. I hope you will do better."

In my experience, my father was all about family. It was just a smaller group. Me and him. With an older sister as formidable as Hyacinth, I could understand why he might have wanted to get out from under the family thumb.

"Ember and Marley are welcome to live with me," Aster said. "We have spare rooms."

"We all have spare rooms," Hyacinth said. "And you have two young children to contend with, Aster. I suspect Ember would be happier living on her own, as that is what she is accustomed to."

"I would prefer that," I said. "Mostly because I can't imagine anyone wanting to pick up after us. Marley and I are fairly sloppy."

Marley glared at me. "You're the sloppy one, Mom. I'm the one always picking up after you."

Heat rose to the back of my neck. "Kids say the darndest things."

Once dinner was finished, the silver platters floated back into the kitchen and were promptly replaced by dessert. Marley's eyes grew the size of walnuts when she saw the chocolate cake that landed nearby her on the table.

"We call that the Devil's Mud," Linnea said, noticing Marley's interest.

"I can see why," I said.

"And it tastes as moist as it looks," Florian said.

Marley and I cringed simultaneously.

"What's the matter?" Aster inquired. "Do you not like chocolate cake?"

"It isn't that," I said. "It's the word Florian used to describe it."

"What? Moist?"

My hands flew to my ears as did Marley's. We both groaned in unison.

"Such an odd reaction to a word," Aunt Hyacinth observed. "Whatever is wrong with moist?"

I squeezed my eyes closed. "Stop saying the word. I don't know why we dislike it, but we do. It just sounds gross."

"Stunting your magic seems to have also stunted your maturity," Aunt Hyacinth observed.

I opened my eyes and fixed them on her. "No, I think that has more to do with having a child when I was still a child."

Some people grew into motherhood out of necessity. Others, like me, bumbled along and hoped for the best. I was still waiting to enter adulthood.

"I think they should live in the guest cottage on the estate," Aster said. "That way we can look after them, but they'll have their own space."

"That's an excellent idea," Linnea agreed.

Florian made a disgruntled noise. "I thought I was going to be able to move into the guest cottage."

Aunt Hyacinth fixed her intimidating gaze on him and I felt myself shrinking in my seat, even though it wasn't directed at me. "I've told you before, Florian. When you prove yourself to be a worthy Rose-Muldoon, then you will reap the benefits of such an association."

Florian slumped in his seat. "It isn't fair. They haven't had to prove anything. They haven't even proved their bloodline yet."

"You know as well as anyone that the proof is just a

formality at this point." Aunt Hyacinth's expression grew pinched. She was clearly ill at ease having this conversation at the table. "Besides, it's only fitting that they should live there. After all, it was the place where your cousin was born."

"Her father lost his claim on it when he left," Florian complained.

Aunt Hyacinth glared at him. "Please don't make our guests feel unwelcome. We've waited a long time to find Yarrow...pardon me, Ember, and I'll not have them disappearing because you behaved like a selfish, spoiled brat."

Florian tossed his linen napkin onto the table and stomped out of the room like a selfish, spoiled brat. Aunt Hyacinth was tough, but she wasn't wrong.

"Tell me how my brother died, would you?" she asked. "It's bothered me, not knowing."

"You knew he died?" I queried.

She nodded. "I felt the change in the wind. It was eleven years ago, yes?"

"Yes." A year before Marley was born. It still pained me that he never got to meet her.

As though reading my mind, Aunt Hyacinth glanced over at my daughter, who was happily eating her chocolate cake.

She smiled faintly. "Trust me, my dear, he would have approved."

CHAPTER 5

"Welcome to Rose Cottage," Linnea said.

I stood in front of the charming home in complete silence. It could not possibly be a real house. A real house that I was born in, that my parents lived in, and that Marley and I would now occupy.

"I can see where it got its name," I said, noting the blooming rose bushes that gathered around the wrought iron fence. There were pink, red, and even some coral-colored roses in the mix.

"Don't be fooled," Linnea said. "The cottage was named after our family. The flowers are just a nice touch."

Marley grabbed me by the hand. "Can we see the inside?"

"In a minute," I said. I was still drinking in the scene. It wasn't every day I felt like I'd stepped into a fairytale. In my experience, disappointment waited on the other side of that pretty painted door.

"It is perfect, isn't it?" Marley said wistfully.

The brick house was symmetrical, with white windows and dormers above the top two windows. The arched door hovered somewhere between sage green and cream. The doorway protruded slightly and formed almost a triangle shape. The mismatched bricks in the front only enhanced its charm.

"Mom, there's a chimney," Marley said, pointing upward. "That means there's a fireplace, right?"

"I guess so," I said. I knew zilch about managing a fireplace. I didn't even like to use the Aim 'n Flame on a candle. For someone whose name meant 'dying fire,' I wasn't too keen on handling flames, and certainly not after my run-in with Jimmy the Lighter.

"Why don't I open the front door and you can explore?" Linnea said.

Marley could hardly stand still. She hopped beside me like a caffeinated rabbit. We followed Linnea inside and I stopped short, wiping the disbelief from my eyes. This was going to be our home. What had I done in life to deserve a home like this?

"Well, I can see why Florian is upset," I said. "This place is fantastic."

Linnea gave a dismissive flick of her fingers. "Don't mind Florian. His place in the main house is three times the size of the cottage. He's used to getting his own way is all, but he won't hold it against you. He's far too lazy to hold a grudge."

That was good news, except for the lazy part. I didn't want to alienate the first cousin I'd ever had. Or at least it should take longer than a day to annoy him.

"What are the floors made of?" I asked. There was no carpet, only attractive area rugs.

"This one is made of flagstone," Linnea replied. "You'll be pleased to know it's easy to clean and very robust. Perfect for a dog and a child."

"And Mom," Marley added. "She's the one most likely to drop something."

I examined the light gray flooring. "It's like something in a magazine." Much better than the puke green carpet in our apartment.

"The rest of the cottage has wooden floors," Linnea said. "The flagstone is only in the entryway and the kitchen."

Marley glanced upward. "Those wooden beams on the ceiling are really cool. I've never seen anything like them."

Linnea smiled. "They're very typical of cottages here."

"And look at all those built-in bookshelves," Marley said, her voice rising. She ran over to inspect the books.

"We can remove those books, if you like," Linnea said.

"No," Marley said sharply. "We keep the books, right?"

"It depends on what kind of books they are," I said. "They need to be appropriate for your age." Just because she could read at an adult level didn't mean she was allowed to read adult books. She was only ten, after all.

"Would you like to see the kitchen?" Linnea asked.

"I would," Marley said. "Mom's not much of a cook. As long as there's a microwave, though, we'll manage."

I didn't need my cousin to know all of my shortcomings in one day. She deserved time to be disappointed in me.

"Maybe it's because I didn't have the right kitchen," I said airily. "Maybe now I'll want to cook." I shot her an accusatory look. "But only if someone decides to expand her palate beyond the breaded food group."

I followed Linnea into the kitchen and gasped. I'd never seen a more pleasant place to cook in my life. The cabinets were a pale blue with butcher-block countertops. The sink was enormous and deep with a curved silver faucet. A decorative heart adorned the wall above the sink.

"Is that made from straw?" I asked, gesturing to the heart.

Linnea wore an amused expression. "No, it's made from a willow tree. Your mother made it, in fact. Mother says she was very crafty."

"Nothing like me then." The closest I came to crafts was a Popsicle stick with googly eyes.

I touched the heart and my own heart began to pound. My mother had made this with her own two hands. Amazing.

"This kitchen is way too nice," I said. "I don't think I'll be able to use it for cooking. I wouldn't want to mess it up."

"That's why cleaning is necessary," Linnea said.

Marley laughed. "Good luck with that."

"Have you really never been in a kitchen like this before?" Linnea asked, amazed.

I shook my head. "Most people I know live in apartments. The kitchens I've been in definitely did not look like this."

"The house has been updated since your parents lived here," Linnea said. "But the original features like the floors and the beams have been here since the house was built." She surveyed the room. "There's still a lot of good energy here. Can you feel it?"

"I don't know," I said. "I think it's a great house, but it's hard to forget that my mother died here."

Linnea's expression clouded over. "Of course. I didn't mean to imply…"

"It's all good," I interjected.

Prescott Peabody III ran into the room, sniffing excitedly. He seemed perfectly content to stay here.

"I think we have PP3's seal of approval," Marley said.

I glanced down nervously. "Why? Did he pee?"

Marley lifted him into her arms. "No, he's wagging his tail. He seems happy."

Phew.

"Once you're settled," Linnea said, "I would love it if you came for dinner one night this week to meet my children."

Marley lit up. "You have kids?"

Linnea smoothed the hair on Marley's head. "Well, they're

not as young as you. Not anymore. Bryn is fourteen and Hudson is thirteen."

"Hudson?" I queried. "How did you get away with a name like that?" It sounded way too normal.

Linnea pursed her lips. "My ex-husband isn't a wizard. Wyatt's a werewolf and he insisted his son have a more masculine name."

A werewolf? I gulped.

"Oh, I didn't realize you were divorced," I said, focusing on the part of that sentence I was more comfortable with. "I'm sorry."

"Well, I'm not sorry," she said. "Best day of my life was when I signed the papers."

"That's good then," I said.

"Don't worry," Linnea said. "You'll get the chance to meet him. And I'm sure he'll hit on you when you do. Why should his habits stop just because he isn't married to me anymore?"

"He'll only hit on me once," I said. "He'll get the message loud and clear that I'm not interested."

Marley nodded solemnly. "Mom can be very loud and very clear."

Linnea gave me a tired smile. "The children adore him. He's a good dad and that's the main thing. Truth be told, the rest of it is white noise now."

"So are you seeing anyone special now?" I asked.

She barked a short laugh. "In all my spare time? I'm a single mom running a business, while trying to keep the Rose-Muldoon name out of the mud. No, I have no time to see anyone special. Besides, Mother would have a fit if I dated without her blessing again. She never forgave me for Wyatt."

"You didn't have her blessing?" I queried.

"Stars and stones, that's an understatement," she said. "We eloped. I was pretty sure I'd be written out of the will at that point. Once the marriage started to go south, Mother came around and I was welcomed back into the family."

"It sounds like it lasted a reasonable amount of time, though," I said. "The marriage."

Linnea shrugged. "Twelve years. Probably five more years than the marriage deserved. I tried to keep going for the sake of the children, but eventually I realized that I wasn't doing them any favors. There was always underlying tension in the house. It became unbearable."

"Well, we'd be happy to come for dinner any night you want us," I said. It would be nice for Marley to meet her cousins. Even though they were slightly older, they would be helpful in showing her the ropes in Starry Hollow.

"How about I check the schedule and let you know?"

"Sounds good," I said. "Where do you live?"

"I run an inn over on Acacia Street," she said. "The children and I live on the lower level. The rest of the house is devoted to the business."

"Do you do all the cooking there?" I asked.

"Not all," Linnea said. "I do love to cook, though. I'd be happy to show you how to make a few things, if you're interested."

"She is," Marley said quickly. Too quickly.

"I think it would be great if we both learned a few recipes," I said. Marley was certainly old enough and mature enough to learn her way around a kitchen.

"Wonderful," Linnea said. "The children will be so excited to meet you. They've never met anyone from New Jersey before."

"Tell them to count their blessings," I said.

Linnea closed the door behind her, leaving Marley and I alone to explore the rest of the cottage. I was still reeling from the fact that I was born here. That my mother died here.

"Mom, come see my room," Marley called.

I followed the sound of her voice to an upstairs bedroom. The walls were made of white shiplap and an old-fashioned brass bed stood in the middle of the room, covered in a colorful quilt. Marley sat on the bed, admiring the quilt.

"It's so pretty," Marley said. "I can't believe we get to live here."

I sat beside her on the bed. "I'll need to look for a job as soon as possible. There's no way we can afford to live here, certainly not if I'm unemployed."

"But, Mom, weren't you listening?" Marley said. "This is technically your house. It belonged to your dad."

I glanced around the room. "I feel a little guilty about Florian. He seems to think he's entitled to it."

Marley waved a dismissive hand. "Like Linnea said, he gets to keep living in that enormous mansion. He'll be fine."

"Look at you, Miss Marley. To the manor born."

She stretched out on the bed and I moved beside her.

"Does this mean you might actually sleep in your own bed from now on?" I asked hopefully.

She kissed the tip of my nose. "I don't know. I haven't seen your room yet."

I laughed and let her snuggle against me. Despite all the beauty and charm in this house, there was no better feeling in the world than being loved by your kid.

"Can't we wait another few days before enrolling you in school?" I asked, bright and early the next morning.

Marley fixed me with her hard stare. "Mom, you're supposed to be the one encouraging me to start school as soon as possible. Why would you want to put it off?"

The truth was that I wanted to enjoy the time with Marley in our new home. It was such a nice change from the dumpy apartment. Without a job at the moment, I also didn't have the stress of work on my shoulders. Of making ends meet. On the other hand, Marley did love school. It wasn't fair to deprive her of an education for my own selfish purposes.

"Fine," I said, relenting. "I'm ready when you are."

Marley gave PP3 a scratch behind the ears. "Let's go then."

I groaned. "At least we can walk. That's a nice change."

Marley's eyes shone. "It really is. I won't miss riding the bus one bit." She hooked the lead on the dog's collar. "It will be great exercise for PP3. Maybe he'll lose a few pounds."

I clapped my hands over the dog's ears. "Marley Rose, don't be insensitive. He doesn't need to lose weight. He looks good just the way he is."

Marley rolled her eyes. "Mom, stop confusing yourself with the dog. We talked about this."

I slipped on my shoes and grabbed the keys to the cottage. "I guess the exercise will be good for me, too."

We walked across the grounds of the estate until we reached the public sidewalk that led into town.

"My legs are tired," I complained. "How far did you say the walk is?"

Marley shook her head. "Your legs can't possibly be tired already. The distance to school is only 0.7 of a mile."

"Yes, but I have to walk back, too. That's..." I mentally calculated.

"1.4 miles, Mom," Marley finished for me.

"I was just about to say that," I said. Math had never been my strong suit.

Once I got over the initial shock of 1.4 miles a day, I realized that the walk itself was pleasant. I'd noticed upon arrival what a pretty town Starry Hollow was, but the walk to school confirmed it. In all honesty, it wouldn't be a bad way to start each day. Even PP3 seemed excited by the prospect.

He only barked once at a bird that had the audacity to land on the sidewalk in front of us. Beyond that, he seemed to be in a walking stupor. We were all high on Starry Hollow.

"There are so many places I want to go," Marley said. "It's like the best outdoor mall in the world."

Although it was far from a mall in appearance, I knew what she meant. The town seemed to have everything we could possibly want or need, as well as places we didn't.

"What kind of store is Spellcaster's?" Marley asked.

I peered at the window display from across the street. "Looks like they sell wands. I guess school supplies will take on a whole new meaning next year."

We looked at each other and laughed. It was all so surreal.

"Can we go in Elixir?" she asked.

I gave the building the once-over. "Not until you're twenty-one, or whatever the drinking age is. Elixir is a cocktail bar."

Marley pointed excitedly to another shop a few doors down. "That place is called Quicksilver. They actually sell broomsticks!"

"I guess somebody has to," I replied.

"Oh, Mom, I really want to see inside."

"We live here now," I said. "There will be plenty of time to hit up every shop and examine every broomstick."

Marley glanced up at me. "Do you think we'll be happy here?"

"You know as well as I do that happiness isn't a permanent condition," I said. "It's a temporary feeling. This too shall pass."

Her face fell. "I think that's what you're supposed to say when things are rough, not when things are good."

I sighed. "In my experience, it's the other way around." I felt a little guilty for being negative around Marley, but I didn't want her to grow up believing the world was an ideal place. As far as I was concerned, that was a dangerous precedent.

"I love that I can hear the ocean from here," Marley said.

She was right. Although there was no view from where we stood, the sound of the waves crashing against the shore carried inland. It was a surprisingly soothing sound.

"Can we go to that ice cream place after school?" Marley asked. She pointed to a Cedar-shake building with a sign that read Stars and Cones.

"We'll see," I replied. "Maybe it'll be your treat for surviving your first day of a new school."

Marley laughed. "Surviving? Mom, you forget that I'm the one who's excited."

"I don't forget," I said. "I just don't understand it."

About twenty minutes later, we arrived at Starry Hollow Middle School. I blamed PP3 for the slow speed. The school was surprisingly attractive with breezeways and lots of open space.

We opened the double doors and stepped into the bright and airy corridor. A sign directed us to the administrative offices. Upon first glance, the woman behind the desk looked like your quintessential school secretary. Her brown hair was streaked with gray and she wore a frumpy floral blouse with a misguided bow. Then I noticed her wings.

Marley gasped. "Mom, she must be a fairy."

The woman glanced up sharply. "Can I help you?"

I stepped up to the counter. "Yes, I'm here to enroll my daughter in school. She's new in town."

The woman peered at us. "I have no paperwork for a new student."

"That's why I'm here," I said. "To fill out paperwork. If you'll just hand me the forms, I'll be out of your hair in a jiffy. I'm a master form-filler-inner."

The woman was not amused. "I can't simply allow the student to enroll without the appropriate paperwork."

"But that's why I'm here. To complete the appropriate paperwork." I felt the tension growing in my shoulders. Marley must have sensed it, too, because she pinched my arm.

"Mom, don't go Jersey on her," she whispered. "Please."

I stuffed down any impulse to be difficult. For Marley's sake, I forced a smile. "I have a ten-year-old daughter who should be attending school here. If you would kindly tell me how to best facilitate this, I solemnly swear to follow your instructions to a T."

The woman's wings fluttered, seemingly in annoyance. "Do you have a passport or some type of identification?"

I whipped out my wallet and placed my driver's license on the counter. The woman examined it closely.

"Do you have identification that shows your new address?"

"No," I said. "This whole thing sort of happened quickly and there hasn't been time…"

The woman slid the license back toward me. "Unless you have official documents that show your new Starry Hollow residence, I'm afraid I can't help you."

"But my license is New Jersey," I said. "Clearly, I'm not trying to sneak her into a better school district all the way from there. We live here now."

The fairy was unrelenting. "Be that as it may, I need proper identification and proper paperwork before I can admit a new student. Rules are rules."

I felt Marley's fingers dig into my wrist. She really did not want me to make a scene in her new school. As much as it irked me, I understood and held my tongue.

"Okay," I said. "Then we'll be back shortly with whatever you need."

As I turned to leave, the secretary called after us, "And next time, please leave your dog outside. Pets are not permitted inside the school. They upset the shifter children."

"Got it," I called over my shoulder.

Marley shot me a wary look. "The shifter children?"

"I guess Starry Hollow has more than just werewolves," I said, as though that was a perfectly reasonable statement to make.

Marley pushed open the school door. "Life has gotten really weird."

"You're telling me." We stepped into the sunshine and I looked down at the scruffy Yorkie. "PP3, I don't think we're in Kansas anymore."

CHAPTER 6

AUNT HYACINTH WAS LESS than pleased when I told her about the kerfuffle at the middle school. We were in the main house in a room she dubbed the parlor room.

"Didn't you tell her your name?" Aunt Hyacinth asked. "Did she not know who you were?"

To call my aunt incensed was putting it mildly.

"I didn't have a chance," I said. "She shut me down. I gave her my license, but I guess she didn't really pay attention to my last name. She was too focused on the address."

"This is absurd," Aunt Hyacinth said. "This is why inheriting your mother's coloring is problematic." She rang her little silver bell until Simon appeared. "Simon, I'd like a starburst martini, please. Straight up."

A light alcoholic refreshment at…nine-thirty in the morning.

Simon returned with a drink on a silver tray in the blink of an eye. Talk about efficient.

"Thank you, Simon. I'm going to call the superintendent right now," Aunt Hyacinth said. "This simply cannot stand. It's an affront to the whole family."

"Please don't do that," Marley said. "I don't want to be known as a troublemaker when I haven't even started school yet."

Aunt Hyacinth looked down her nose at Marley. "Marley Rose, you don't seem to understand your position in this town. *You* do not wait for official documentation to enroll in school. Now that they've mentioned it, though, I will arrange for your passports. I should've gotten started on them already."

"Passports?" I queried.

"Paranormals use special passports," she said. "We're not subject to the same jurisdictions as the human world."

That was good to know. I guess that explained why Marley and I couldn't find the town on Google maps. We'd mapped the distance to school using a printed town map we found in the kitchen drawer.

Aunt Hyacinth rang the bell again and Simon appeared with a cell phone on a silver tray. She plucked the phone from the tray and he disappeared once more. They seemed to have some kind of crazy mental telepathy going on.

"Good morning, I'd like to speak to Stanley, please. This is Hyacinth Rose-Muldoon."

"Watch and learn," I whispered to Marley.

"Stanley, yes, a pleasure to hear your voice, too. Listen, my niece attempted to enroll her daughter in the middle school today and was rebuffed in a most demeaning fashion. I'd like that rectified immediately. This child is ridiculously intelligent and needs to be in school." She paused to listen to his reply. "Oh, well aren't you sweet? Yes, of course I'll come. Wouldn't miss it for the world. Give my regards to Hattie." She clicked off the phone and set it back on the tray. "You are free to go back now, if you wish. I'll have my driver take you."

"I think driving would be good," I said. "PP3 is a bit worn out from the walk earlier."

"I'll have someone return him to the cottage," Aunt Hyacinth said. "Would you like me to accompany you to the school, my dear, in case they give further difficulties?"

"No, that's okay," I said. "I'm usually pretty good at handling problems." Except when my daughter muzzled me. Now I had to have my estranged aunt do my dirty work. I didn't like that outcome.

"The car is waiting for you out front then," she said.

"Thank you, Aunt Hyacinth," Marley said.

"Yes, thank you," I added quickly. I didn't want to seem ungrateful.

We returned to the school and I had a brief, shining moment where I felt like Julia Roberts in *Pretty Woman*, returning to the store that had previously rejected her. I longed to walk up to the counter and say to the fairy, "Big mistake. Huge." But I didn't. Instead, I walked up to the counter and said, "We're here to enroll my daughter in school today."

The same secretary fell over herself to assist us. "Yes, of course. I am so sorry about the earlier mix-up."

I didn't bother to point out that there was no mix-up.

"If you'll just hand me the forms, I can get started on the paperwork," I said.

"Oh, that's all been taken care of," the secretary said. "My name is Darlene. If there is anything I can do for you, please let me know."

Wow. Talk about a 180. "Thanks. I think we're good for now."

"Marley will be joining Mr. Fuller's class. I have a student coming down now to escort her to the classroom."

Marley's excitement was palpable. Most kids would have been sick to their stomachs with nerves, but not Marley.

"What happens now?" I asked her. "Do I kiss you on the cheek and run out the door?"

"No kiss, but no running out the door either," Marley replied. "Knowing you, you'll knock someone over. Probably the principal."

She had a point. "Good luck today, sweetheart."

She glared at me. "Don't call me sweetheart. It's demeaning."

"It's a term of endearment," I argued.

She gave me a gentle shove. "I'll see you at the end of the day."

I left the office and wandered down the corridor to the front door, resisting the urge to look back. Marley was so mature for her age. I had no idea where she got it from, certainly not from me.

I'd told the driver not to wait, so I walked home from the middle school, taking time to indulge my thoughts. If nothing else, I sorely needed the exercise after last night's dinner.

I passed the rows of stores from this morning and crossed the road to head toward the residential area of town. There were so many trees here, which was surprising for a seaside town. I expected water, sand, and concrete, but Starry Hollow seemed to have a little bit of everything—trees, cliffs, a river. No wonder it was a sought-after tourist destination for paranormals.

I spotted a path to my right that led into the woods. I was pretty sure that Rose Cottage was in this general direction. If I could find a shortcut, that would make the walk to and from school easier. PP3 might enjoy a stroll through the forest every day. He wasn't a city dog exactly, but he certainly had minimal experience with woodland creatures.

The farther I walked, the less light there was. I was amazed how dark it could look at this time in the morning. Live oaks towered over me, the thick, twisted branches and Spanish moss creating a protective canopy overhead. It was so quiet in here, eerily quiet. The only sound I heard was the crunching of leaves and pebbles beneath my feet. I wondered how often anyone passed this way.

My body jerked at the slightest unexpected noise and I laughed at myself. Starry Hollow was a far cry from New Jersey. These woods were probably one of the safest places on the eastern seaboard. Seriously. This town was nothing short of magical. Literally. A beach. A forest. An enchanted cottage. Okay, so far it was just a cottage, but we were witches, after all. There was bound to be enchantment somewhere in that house.

I picked up the pace, eager to find my way back to the cottage. Prescott Peabody III was probably unhappy being left alone in a strange place for so long. It was one thing to hang out in the apartment all day. He was used to that environment. Although the cottage was a hundred times nicer, it was still foreign to him. It didn't have his usual places to curl up and snooze. Like Marley, though, I was confident that he would adjust.

Birdsong in the trees drew my attention skyward. When was the last time I listened to the sound of birds? I couldn't even remember. Although the change was sudden and bizarre, I was pleased for Marley—that I would be able to give her the magical childhood that she deserved. She was an amazing kid and I was so lucky to have her.

A flash of white on the ground ahead caught my eye. What was that? It looked like someone had left their laundry in the middle of the woods. Maybe teenagers came to party here at night. As I moved closer to investigate, my heart began to pound in my chest. This was not someone's laundry. This was a white dress.

I froze when I realized the horror of the situation. It wasn't *just* a white dress.

Someone was wearing it.

I rushed forward and dropped to my knees. A young woman was sprawled on the ground in front of me, her face turned to the side.

"Are you okay?" I asked. What a stupid question. Of course she wasn't okay. She was on the ground in the middle of the forest all by herself.

I turned her head toward me. Her skin was pale and her eyes were…open. I grabbed her wrist and felt for a pulse. The only time in my life I'd done this was on a mannequin in health class in high school. I wasn't even good at it then. I was pretty sure the mannequin died because of my ineptitude.

I felt…nothing.

I touched her forehead, the way I did when I suspected Marley had a fever. The girl's skin was cold. So very cold. I had no way of knowing how long she'd been here, but she certainly wasn't walking out. Not unless the dead walked around here, which suddenly seemed entirely possible.

I glanced helplessly around the forest. I wasn't strong enough to carry her. I didn't even know how far I needed to go for help. I had only guessed that this was a shortcut to the cottage.

I gazed at her pretty face. I hated to leave her here, but I had no choice.

"I'll be back with help," I told her. "I promise." I stood and began to run. I ran like a disgruntled car owner was chasing me. I leapt over fallen logs and grazed my bare legs on brambles. Finally, I reached a familiar sight.

Rose Cottage stood nestled in the trees ahead. I wasn't sure at what point I crossed over on to my family's property. I would have to ask where the border was. Of course, I didn't need Rose Cottage. I needed someone in the main house to call the police. I breathed a sigh of relief when I saw a familiar figure in the distance.

"Florian," I called, waving my arms dramatically. He was in the field with...Was that a gun? He took aim at the sky and fired. What on earth was he shooting at? Something plunged to the earth. Whatever he was aiming for, he managed to hit it.

I raced across the open field, calling his name. When I got close enough, I realized that he was wearing earplugs. He removed them when he saw me.

"Ember," he said, scrutinizing me. "I thought you were at school with Marley."

"I took the scenic route home," I said, panting. "I need help."

He didn't hesitate. "What can I do?"

"I need you to call the police."

His brow lifted. "The sheriff? Why?"

"Because there's a dead body in the woods. I think a girl has been murdered."

CHAPTER 7

I DIDN'T RETURN to the woods after Florian called the sheriff. I hung around the cottage, trying to keep busy but wondering what had happened to that poor girl. Florian had promised to update me, so when I heard a knock at the door, I assumed he'd come back with a full report.

I yanked open the door and saw no one.

"Ahem," a voice said.

I glanced down to see a little man, no higher than my waist, wearing a Stetson. His skin had a greenish hue.

"Are you Miss Ember Rose?" the little man asked.

Before I could stop myself, I blurted, "Sweet baby Elvis, you're adorable." I slapped my hand over my mouth.

His beady eyes grew to slits. "Adorable? I am the Deputy Sheriff in Starry Hollow, I'll have you know. I am as far from adorable as you can get." He put his little hands on his little hips and I nearly burst into laughter. I could just imagine him trying to assert his authority in New Jersey. Elementary school kids would use him as a volleyball. And not even the tough kids.

"I beg your pardon," I said, quickly trying to recover. "How can I help you, Deputy? Is this about the girl I found?"

He tipped back his hat, which only made his head look smaller. "Yes, ma'am. I need to bring you down to Sheriff Nash's office for questioning, if you don't mind."

"Well, actually I do mind. I'm in the middle of redecorating." True, my idea of redecorating meant moving a chair from one side of the room to another, but still.

"I don't think I made myself clear," the deputy said. "It's not a request."

"Yes, of course. I'm the one who found her. He probably needs to ask me questions about the crime scene or something." I'd been a witness to a robbery when I was younger and I still remembered having to go down to the station to identify the suspect in the lineup. Even though I'd known at the time he couldn't see through the one-way mirror, it was still an unsettling experience.

"Do you know how long this will take? My daughter is at her first day of school and I want to be there to pick her up. She's very anxious."

"I really couldn't say," the deputy said. "But don't worry about your daughter. We'll make sure one of your family members collects her, if need be."

I didn't think much of it, considering how early it still was in the day. How long could a few questions take?

We walked out to the driveway and I was surprised when he opened the back door of the car for me.

"Don't be ridiculous," I said. "You're not a taxi service. I'll sit in the front."

He gave me a strange look, but said nothing as I slipped into the passenger seat. I wasn't surprised to see that the driver's side had been manipulated so that he could reach both the pedals and the steering wheel at the same time.

"So…" I began. How to broach this topic? "I'm going to go

out on a limb here and say you're a leprechaun." Subtlety was not my specialty.

"However did you fit inside this car with that massive brain of yours?" he shot back.

Touché. I liked him already.

"So what's it like being a leprechaun?" I asked. "I only ask because you're the first one I've ever met in real life."

He grimaced. "Our kind has suffered immensely in the last century. Popular entertainment has sullied our good name. Meanwhile, vampires have become sexy." He shook his head in disgust. "I don't know how that ever happened. Back in the day, vampires were nothing more than predators in the animal food chain."

"You sound a little bitter there, Deputy," I said. "But look at you. You've got this tough guy thing going on. You're wearing the cool hat. You're doing your part to improve the leprechaun image."

"Don't patronize me, ma'am," he said, his gaze fixed on the road. "I may be small and green, but I'm sharp as a unicorn horn."

"Are they sharp?" I queried. "I would imagine them being a little blunt at the top. Like an orange traffic cone."

He cast a sidelong glance at me. "Has anyone ever told you you're a bit odd?"

I straightened in my seat. This remark coming from a little green man in a Stetson.

"So tell me about the sheriff," I said. "I've never met a real sheriff before either. I picture some old, white-haired dude who started when Hyacinth was a baby. Probably doesn't leave the office much anymore. Sends his minions out to pick up witnesses and do all of the investigating. Am I right?"

"Are you calling me a minion?" he asked sharply.

"Hey, it's not an insult. I was a minion for Hilda Santiago. There's no shame in minionhood. Besides, if the sheriff is old and crotchety, then you'll graduate to his job when he finally pops off."

The deputy suppressed a smile. "I'll let you judge that for yourself."

The sheriff was not an old, white-haired dude. In fact, I would go so far as to say he was downright hot. Sheriff Granger Nash was about six feet tall, with a glorious head of dark brown hair—the kind of hair that made girls want to run their fingers through it. Not my fingers, of course. Just girls in general.

The sheriff swaggered into the room with an attitude I hadn't seen since I watched a John Wayne movie as a teenager. I waited for him to announce that it would be pistols at high noon.

"So you're Ember Rose. Is that right?" He narrowed his eyes, as though studying me with half-closed eyes was a better option.

"I am," I said. "And judging from that shiny gold star on your shirt, you must be the sheriff."

He glanced down at the star pinned to his shirt as though he'd never seen it before. "Oh, is that what the star badge means? I always thought it was a reward for a job well done. I have another one at home that says 'Didn't Murder Anyone Today. Good job.'"

"Is that so, Sheriff Nash?" Sheriff Smartass more like. "I'm not really sure how things are done here in Scary Hollow, but I'd think murder-by-sheriff was off the menu."

"Starry Hollow," he corrected me with a trace of annoyance. "Your family tells me that you had no knowledge of your magic until recently."

I nodded. "That's right. When my life was in jeopardy, I snapped."

His curiosity was piqued. "You snapped?"

"Yep. Out came the powers, like the Hulk, but less violent. It was pretty cool, actually."

"I wouldn't know," he said darkly.

"You're not a wizard?" I asked. "You have that weird look, like you might be."

He snorted. "Weird? You really shouldn't call the sheriff weird. It's just bad manners."

And pretty stupid. I'd only arrived in town yesterday. The last thing I wanted to do was rub the sheriff the wrong way.

"Why don't we step into the interview room so we can have some privacy?" he said. "Can I offer you anything to drink?"

"Aren't you supposed to make me thirsty?" I joked. "That way I'll confess faster."

He narrowed his eyes again. "Do you have something to confess, Miss Rose?"

"No, sorry," I said. "I was just trying to lighten the mood."

His expression remained serious. "You discovered the dead body of a young lady this morning, Miss Rose. Do you really think we need to lighten the mood?"

I shifted uncomfortably. He was right. He just didn't understand that when I was nervous, I made jokes. That was how I hid my discomfort.

"Of course not," I mumbled, trailing him into the adjacent room. I sat down at a small table and folded my hands in my lap. Demure seemed the way to go.

"Do you know who the young lady is?" he asked, settling down across from me. His brown eyes gazed at me inquisitively. The long, thick eyelashes were a crime against women everywhere.

"I don't," I said. "But that's not really a surprise, since I hardly know anyone here."

"Yes, because you're new to town. So I've heard."

"My daughter and I are living in Rose Cottage."

"And why is that?" he asked. "Where did you move from?"

"New Jersey," I replied. "There was an incident at work..." I hesitated. I didn't really want to relive my experience with Jimmy the Lighter. "It's a long story. I'd rather not get into it. Needless to say, my cousins found me and here we are."

"The girl's name is Fleur Montbatten. She is...was sixteen years old and a student at Starry Hollow High School."

Nausea rolled over me. I knew she was young, but I didn't realize *how* young. What a waste.

"Was she a witch like us?" I asked.

"I'm not a witch," the sheriff said.

"Oh," I said. "When I said *us*, I meant my family. Not you and me. There is no us, right? That would be ridiculous. We just met." I laughed awkwardly. I knew I was babbling now and felt like a complete idiot.

A smile tugged at the sheriff's lips. "No, I'm fairly confident there is no us."

I studied him. "If you're not a witch and you're clearly not a leprechaun or a fairy, what does that leave?"

"I'm a werewolf."

Well, that explained the strong whiff of masculinity coming my way. "Wow, a real werewolf. I'm meeting all kinds today. So what's that like?"

He gazed at me with a mixture of horror and amusement. "What's that like? I don't even know how to answer that. What's it like being a woman?"

"Really good most days, except that time of the month," I said. "I guess you would know all about that though, being a werewolf."

He opened his mouth to say something, but then snapped it closed. "Why don't we stick to my questions for now?"

"Sounds good to me," I said. "I do have a habit of saying whatever comes to mind, so it's probably best that you set clear boundaries for me." My running mouth got me into trouble on more occasions than I could remember over the years. I certainly didn't want to court trouble now in the sheriff's office.

"Do you know who Fleur Mountbatten is?" he asked.

I didn't understand the question. "Yes, you just told me. Her name was Fleur, which I think means flower in French." If my eighth-grade French class had taught me anything.

He ignored my last comment. "She was the Maiden in the coven. That's an important position to hold."

"The Maiden? That's the title?"

"It is," he said. "A highly coveted title that many witches would like to have. She served as the apprentice to the High Priestess. It's a great honor to be the Maiden."

"So she's a glorified assistant?" I queried. "So what are you suggesting? That someone might have killed her because they wanted her snazzy title?"

He gazed at me intently. "You're new to town. New to the coven. Maybe you want to make a name for yourself?"

The realization of what he was asking settled in. "Wait, you think I killed a sixteen-year-old girl so I could steal her crown."

"Technically, she wore a silver circlet," he said.

Something occurred to me. "So she was sixteen and her title was the Maiden. Doesn't that imply some type of purity?"

"As a matter of fact, it does. The Maiden is always a virgin."

I slapped my hands on the table and burst into laughter. "Well, there's your answer right there. I couldn't possibly have killed her to take her position. I haven't been a Maiden in eleven years." I remained thoughtful for a moment. "Unless there's such a thing as a born-again Maiden. Because it's been a good four years since I've had any action.

I'm not sure how strict the coven is with these requirements."

The sheriff's face turned beet red. He cleared his throat. "Right. That's probably a little more information than I needed, but thank you for your full disclosure."

"You think that was full disclosure? I could go on..."

He waved me off. "Thank you, Miss Rose. I think we're done here for now."

"Are you sure? Because I want to help. If this is going to be my new home, I want to make a positive contribution to society, you know?"

He managed a smile. "How very admirable of you."

"You know, if you'd done your homework, you would've known that I have a ten-year-old daughter. That would have answered your question without all of this interrogation drama."

His expression shifted to one of amusement. "Interrogation drama?"

I waved my hands around the room. "Yes, dragging me down here and putting me in the hot seat. All of this would've been easily avoided if you'd done your due diligence."

He pushed back his chair and stood. "What makes you think I didn't know?"

He walked to the door and held it open for me.

"Because you thought..." I stood in the open doorway. "Oh, I see. You just wanted to take the measure of me, is that it? See how I responded under pressure?"

He grinned. "You talk a lot, that's for sure."

"You don't even know she was murdered. Maybe she tripped and fell in the woods and hit her head."

"Her death was no accident," he said darkly.

I could tell he had more information than he was sharing. "Am I still a suspect then?"

His jaw tightened. "Everyone is a suspect until I've identified the murderer."

"But we've established that I had no motive," I argued.

"The only thing we've established is that you have not been a virgin in over a decade," he said. "I have no idea what other motive you may have had. That's all part of the investigation."

I didn't like the sound of that. "Aunt Hyacinth is not going to be happy about this. I get the feeling that she doesn't like the Rose name under scrutiny."

He snorted again. "You read people pretty well, don't you?"

"It was kind of a necessity where I'm from," I said. "You don't read people well, you end up in trouble."

"If your Aunt Hyacinth has a problem with my investigation, you can tell her to come and talk to me about it. I'm always happy to hear from citizens of Starry Hollow, especially bluebloods like descendants of the One True Witch."

I could tell by the way he said *Aunt Hyacinth* that he didn't approve of my family. It was easy to guess why. Sheriff Granger Nash was a werewolf in a town mostly comprised of witches. Hyacinth Rose-Muldoon was the *de facto* leader of the town. She and the sheriff probably butted heads regularly.

"What's the One True Witch?" I asked.

His eyes grew round. "They haven't told you about your heritage yet? Fancy that. It's one of the qualities that makes your family so darned special. Your bloodline can be traced straight back to the very first witch, or so the legend goes."

How about that? "Then I guess I can cancel my ancestry.com account."

He seemed mildly amused. "Guess so."

"Well, if you have any more questions for me, you know

where to find me," I said. "Maybe next time come yourself. I don't think your deputy likes me very much."

He arched an eyebrow. "And what makes you think I do?"

"Like I said, I read people pretty well. I guess that includes werewolves."

Before he could respond, I sailed out the door.

CHAPTER 8

I'D NEVER STAYED in a bed and breakfast before, so I didn't know what to expect when we arrived at Linnea's inn. Palmetto House was striking from the outside—from the blue wrought iron balconies to the Silver Moon flag that hung proudly from the second floor. Colorful flowers were woven into the scalloped wrought iron.

We each took a different set of stairs and met on the front porch.

"That's awesome," Marley said. Sometimes it was life's simple pleasures. Like a symmetrical set of stairs.

"Should we just go inside?" I wasn't sure what the etiquette was when someone lived in an inn.

We didn't need to speculate because Linnea appeared in the doorway. Her white-blond hair was pulled back in an unkempt braid. She wore a gray sleeveless top with black capris and black flip-flops. She looked far removed from the elegant Rose-Muldoon cousin I'd met in my apartment. Then again, she was in her natural habitat now.

"Welcome to Palmetto House," Linnea said, ushering us

inside. "This is the main floor where we greet guests of the inn."

"It's very nice," I said. It really was. The decor was tasteful with a parquet floor and traditional throw rugs. The marble fireplace was the centerpiece of the room. Above it hung a gilded mirror flanked by sconces. A large bouquet of flowers sat in a vase in the middle of the mantel. Everything was carefully appointed.

"This place is huge," I said. "How many rooms does it have?"

"Fifteen," she replied. "We get a fair amount of tourist traffic here because of the location. Paranormals love the seaside just as much as humans do. We also get our share of business travelers."

"Is it full now?" I asked.

"Only half," she said. "I have staff to help me when things are busy. When it's only a few occupants, I handle things myself."

Marley seemed enamored. "So will we get to eat dinner with your guests?"

Linnea smiled at her. "I'm afraid not. We'll eat in the residential part of the house with my kids." She hesitated. "Hopefully, they've cleaned up like I asked them to."

We went down a back staircase to the lower level. Linnea flashed an apologetic look over her shoulder.

"I've been so busy upstairs today, I haven't had a chance to monitor life down here. It's a crapshoot as to whether they did as I told them. They're teenagers, you know?"

The staircase emptied out into a main living area. While the decor itself was as tasteful as the rooms above, it was hard to see beyond the clutter. There were stacks of magazines on the tables and shoes everywhere. I half expected her to tell me her children were training as cobblers. How many pairs of shoes did one family need?

Linnea lifted a pair of sneakers from the floor and wrinkled her nose. "Hudson plays every sport under the sun. He seems to need a different uniform and pair of shoes for each activity. It's ridiculous."

"You said Hudson is thirteen?" I asked.

"Yes, and already turning into his father, which scares the magic out of me. Bryn is my fourteen-year-old. She's sporty like her brother, but she likes her books, too."

I could tell. There were piles of books jammed into every available space. At least she and Marley would have something in common, despite the age difference.

"Hudson Rose-Nash," she yelled. The sound was so unexpected coming from her elegant frame that my whole body jerked in response. "Get your hairy butt in here and clean up this mess like I told you."

I tried to disguise my amused surprise. This was not the Linnea I'd met at all. She'd definitely been on her best behavior then.

A shaggy-haired boy appeared in the doorway. "What do you mean? I did clean up."

His mother stretched out her arms. "Do you call this cleaned up? It looks like a vampire's nest in here. All that's missing is blood."

Hudson began begrudgingly collecting his pairs of shoes. "You don't know what you're talking about. You've never even seen the inside of a vampire's nest."

"You don't know that," Linnea said. "My younger days were wild. How do you think I ended up with your father?"

It occurred to me that Hudson didn't have the white-blond hair indicative of a Rose. Like Marley and me. I felt an instant connection to him.

Hudson stopped picking up his shoes when he noticed us. "Mom, you didn't tell me the company was here."

"Why do you think I told you to clean up your mess? We're having dinner, remember?"

Hudson frowned. "Are you cooking?"

Her hands flew to her hips. "Don't you start with me, young man. My cooking is excellent. If it wasn't, this inn would not be nearly as successful."

He lifted a pair of sandals. "Tourists don't come for your cooking, Mom. I hate to tell you."

"You don't hate to tell me anything," Linnea retorted. "That's the problem. Where's your sister? Half of this stuff is hers."

"She kept saying one more page," Hudson said. "You know how she gets when she's reading."

Linnea cupped her hands around her mouth and bellowed, "Bryn Rose-Nash, front and center."

Marley and I exchanged glances. A willowy brunette appeared, her hair pulled up in a high ponytail. She had her mother's striking features, but presumably her father's brown eyes and hair.

"Cool, the cousins are here." She closed her book and set it aside. "I'm Bryn. You must be Ember and Marley."

"What are you reading?" Marley asked.

"Oh, that? It's way too old for you. It's a romance novel."

I shot a quizzical look at Linnea. She was allowing her fourteen-year-old daughter to read romance novels? I was no prude, but I was pretty sure they contained a lot of sex. Linnea didn't seem to register her daughter's remark.

"Why don't you two keep your cousins entertained while I get started in the kitchen?" Linnea said, looking a little stressed out.

"Is there anything I can do to help?" I asked. Offers of assistance were not my usual gut response, but Linnea seemed to need a hand.

Her relief was palpable. "Would you mind? I can tell you what you need to do."

"It's no trouble at all," I said. "Marley will be fine in here getting to know her cousins." I assumed.

"Absolutely," Bryn said. "I can show her my room. And Hudson has every video game console imaginable in his, if you like that sort of thing."

I left Marley to the impulses of her teenaged cousins and followed Linnea into the kitchen. This room was just as disorganized as the living space. There were dishes on the counter and cups and mugs scattered everywhere. I couldn't tell which were clean and which were dirty. Yikes. And I thought I was sloppy.

"Is this where you cook for your guests at the inn?" I asked.

She shook her head. "No, there's a bigger kitchen on the main floor. This whole lower level is our private space. It was converted years ago, before we even bought it." She shook her head. "I mean, before *I* even bought it."

"You originally bought this with your ex-husband?"

"We originally bought it together...with *my* money. We fixed up what needed fixing. Then I did all the work while he kept himself busy getting acquainted with all the young women in town."

I couldn't imagine anyone cheating on Linnea. I would have thought her beauty and family name alone would've kept a man in line. If a guy didn't want to be faithful to her, what chance did I have? Karl and I were only married for six years before he died. Who knows? Maybe he would have strayed eventually, too.

"So Bryn and Hudson don't have the Rose coloring," I said. "They're like Marley and me."

She pulled a pan from a lower cupboard and set it on the counter. "They're not members of the coven either."

"Why not? Is it because they're half-breeds?"

"When you have a child with another paranormal, you run the risk of not producing a witch or a wizard. Both of my kids ended up full werewolf. No witch genes." She shrugged. "It happens."

I bet Aunt Hyacinth had a coronary when they were born.

"So they can't do any magic?"

She shook her head ruefully. "Nope. No magical abilities whatsoever. It nearly sent my mother into hibernation for a year after Hudson was born. She thought at least one of them would carry on the Rose genes."

Hang on a hot minute. The gears in my brain began to click. Werewolves. Nash. "Is your ex-husband related to the sheriff?"

Linnea nodded. "Wyatt is Granger's older brother."

"Is that why the sheriff doesn't like our family very much?" I asked. "Because of your divorce?"

"Sticks and wicks, no." She shook her head and more pieces of hair fell from the braid. "Granger never liked the way my family treated his brother. Mostly Mother, as you can imagine. My father stayed out of it, for the most part. He tried to balance my mother." She smiled to herself. "He failed most of the time."

"How long ago did your father die?" I asked.

"About ten years ago," she replied. "He suffered a stroke and went downhill from there."

"I'm sorry," I said. I knew how it felt to lose a father. I was only twenty-eight and I'd already lost mine as well as Marley's dad. Life sucked sometimes.

"At least you married for love," I said, trying to look on the bright side. "You didn't marry another wizard just so you could make your mom happy and have children in the coven."

She bit her lip. "There are days when I regret my choice,

but then I look at my kids and my heart melts. Even when they leave their crap all over the house."

I surveyed the kitchen. "Tell me what you need me to do."

She shifted the cutting board across the counter and placed it in front of me. "There's a knife right there. If you wouldn't mind chopping these peppers, that would be a big help."

"Can't you use magic to make things easier?" I asked. She seemed so harried, I would have thought magic like her mother used would improve the quality of her life.

"To be honest, I use magic a lot, especially for the inn. The thing you'll learn is that magic wipes you out when you use too much of it. Half the reason I'm so tired is because I used magic today to get the inn ready for the influx of guests over the weekend."

I started chopping slowly, careful not to knick myself. "So you have a set amount of energy and then it gets depleted?"

"Something like that," she said. "I should have had you come for dinner on a day when I didn't have to deal with the inn as much. I wasn't thinking when I invited you. I was so eager for you to meet my kids."

"Of course," I said. "It doesn't matter to us. It's not like we've been around magic so long that we expect it." I wished I were more advanced so that I could help her right now. The best I could do was try not to slice off my finger while I chopped.

"What about Aster?" I asked. "Is she married to a wizard?"

Linnea pursed her lips. "Of course she is. Aster does everything right. That's why she's Mother's favorite."

"I guess Florian still has the potential to become her favorite," I said.

Linnea blurted a loud laugh. "He'd have to get his life in order first. He refuses to settle down. Mother would like nothing more than to marry him off to the right sort of witch and produce lots of coven babies."

"So what's stopping him?" I asked.

"It started when our dad died," Linnea said. "Florian became stuck in this man-child state. He's got a Peter Pan complex like I've never seen."

"He's a good-looking guy," I said. "There must be a line of girls wanting to take a crack at marrying him."

Linnea busied herself preparing the roast. "You'd better believe it. It's pretty much a Starry Hollow sport, watching to see which girl catches his eye next."

"Does he only date coven witches?"

"Hardly. I think he avoids them on purpose, just to aggravate Mother. He goes through phases. His paranormal of choice at the moment seems to be fairies."

"With the big smiles and sparkles, I can see the allure. Like strippers with wings."

Linnea laughed. "You're a breath of fresh air, Ember. Do you know that? Mother isn't going to know what to do with you."

"To be fair, she's been nothing but generous. I hope I don't piss her off."

"I hope you don't either. You do not want to see the bad side of Mother. Trust me on that. I saw it for years after I married Wyatt."

Together, we finished preparing dinner and the kids set the table with minimal objection. It was a relaxed affair with lots of plate passing and only two spills—the first was Hudson's glass of milk and the second was my beer. Something called Moonglow. Linnea managed to summon enough magic to clean up the mess. The dinner seemed to restore her energy. Maybe food was fuel for magic as well as the body. I had to remember that. Not that I needed an excuse to eat more.

"How are you enjoying school?" Linnea asked Marley.

"It's great so far," Marley said. "I have Mr. Fuller and he seems like a smart guy."

Hudson nodded. "I had Fuller in the middle school. He was decent."

"So you're both in Starry Hollow High School?" I asked.

They nodded in unison.

"We don't see each other much in school though," Bryn said. "I avoid him as much as possible."

"Suits me fine," Hudson said. "I don't need you and your smelly girlfriends gaping at me."

"No one gapes at you, dog breath," she said.

"No name-calling at the table," Linnea said.

"I take dog breath as a compliment," Hudson said. "At least I don't have a crush on a vampire."

Linnea's brow lifted. "Bryn has a crush on a vampire?"

Bryn folded her arms and glared at her brother. "I do not have a crush on him. He has a crush on me."

"Who is this?" Linnea asked. "Why is this the first time I'm hearing about it?"

"Because you're too busy with the inn to pay attention," Bryn snapped.

Linnea's face fell. She looked genuinely crushed by the accusation.

"Don't act like I don't spend time with you," Linnea said. "Sometimes you make it difficult to *want* to spend time with you."

"Thanks a lot, Hudson," Bryn said. "Now you've made mom upset."

Hudson pushed back his chair. "I'm not the one who started it."

"Did too," Bryn said.

I suddenly was thankful that Marley was an only child. And that I was, too, for that matter. I wondered whether

Linnea had lived through similar interactions with her siblings. Somehow I couldn't see Aunt Hyacinth tolerating this kind of behavior at the table or anywhere else.

"So did either of you know Fleur?" I asked, hoping to steer the subject away from arguments.

"Not me," Hudson said. "She was a junior. She had no interest in mixing with seventh graders."

"She was quiet, but pretty popular," Bryn said. "Hard not to be popular when you looked like her."

"Bryn, you're a stunning girl," Linnea said quickly.

"Not like her or you," Bryn said. "I didn't get the witch genes."

I touched my dark head. "Neither did we."

"Yes, but at least you're still witches," Bryn said. "I didn't get the looks or the magic."

Ah, the angst of a teen girl. Bryn was athletic, pretty, and smart. She had no clue that the odds were already stacked in her favor.

"I knew Fleur from the coven, of course," Linnea said. "The Maiden played a very important role."

"That's what I was told," I said. "Like the shadow to the High Priestess."

Linnea nodded. "The Maiden is chosen very carefully. It's a great honor to serve. And to die from hemlock..."

"Hemlock?" I repeated. "That's the cause of death?"

Linnea nodded. "Mother told me earlier today. They found hemlock in her system. It's a poisonous plant."

"I've heard of it," I said. "Her family must be devastated."

Tears swelled in Linnea's eyes. "I can only imagine their grief." Her gaze darted to Bryn. "Losing a child...It's the worst imaginable fate."

My chest tightened at the thought of losing Marley. Losing Karl and my father had been hard enough. Marley would be pure devastation.

"I hope the sheriff catches the killer soon," Linnea said. "Starry Hollow doesn't need a murderer on the loose, especially one that targets teenaged girls."

"Are you sure we can't use Bryn as bait?" Hudson asked.

Linnea's eyes narrowed at her son. I watched as his cup of milk drifted above his head and tipped, pouring the white liquid all over him. Okay, so three spills total, but only one was deliberate.

"Hey," Hudson objected, wiping his face with his napkin. "No magic at the table."

"It's my table," Linnea said. "I'll do as I please."

She snapped her fingers and a towel appeared on Hudson's head. He used it to wipe off the rest of the milk. Linnea snapped her fingers again and the towel disappeared. I wondered if magic would ever come that easily to me. I'd probably need a wand and a spell book for the rest of my life, One True Witch descendant or not.

"Before I forget," Linnea said, "let me know if you need any help finding a white dress for the induction ceremony."

I nearly choked on my beer. "The what?"

Linnea frowned. "The coven induction ceremony. Hasn't Mother told you?"

"That would be a big, fat no," I said.

"You need to be officially admitted to the coven," Linnea said. "There will be a short ceremony tomorrow night because we need the full moon."

"Then yes," I said. "I can tell you right now I need help finding a white dress, preferably not one with cat faces all over it."

Bryn and Hudson laughed.

"It's atrocious, isn't it?" Bryn said.

Linnea spread her palms flat. "Please, for Nature's sake, no one say anything about the kaftan. Mother loves it."

"Speaking of cats, is yours around?" Marley asked. "I'd love to see it."

"Marley's a big fan of cats," I explained. "Our neighbor, Miss Kowalski, had three."

"No cat, I'm afraid," Linnea said. "I married a werewolf. My kids are werewolves. The last thing this house of chaos needs is an uppity cat."

Fair enough. "Will I have one?" I asked. Because I wasn't sure how PP3 would react to sharing a house with a cat. He was pretty much set in his ways at this point.

"It's not a requirement," Linnea said. "Sometimes the familiar finds you. You've only been here a short while. Maybe there's a familiar out there, waiting for its time."

That sounded too close to stalking for my liking.

Marley, on the other hand, was only too eager to expand our family. "I think PP3 would love a cat buddy."

"Doubtful," I said, "but I'll take it under advisement."

"That's what you say when you mean no," Marley said, pouting.

"I'll make you a deal. If a cat is ballsy enough to walk up to me and form a telepathic connection with the nonsense that bangs around in my head, then she has earned the right to live with us. How about that?"

Marley smiled. "We have a deal."

CHAPTER 9

"LET ME ADJUST YOUR WREATH," Aster said. "If the wind blows hard enough, you'll lose it completely." I stood in my bedroom as Aster and Linnea put the final touches on my ceremony ensemble.

"That's happened to me more times than I can count," Linnea added. "Witches love to show off and blow the wind around. Very atmospheric."

My brow creased. "Wait, the ceremony is actually outside?"

"Of course it is," Aster replied. "What did you expect?"

"A cozy indoor gymnasium? A banquet room at a local hotel?"

The sisters laughed.

"We're called the Silver Moon coven," Linnea said. "All of our major events take place under the watchful gaze of the moon and stars."

"So that's why the Maiden's hat was silver with that circle in the front?" I queried.

"It's not a hat, silly," Aster said. "It's a circlet."

I snapped my fingers. "That's right. A circlet. It reminds me of Wonder Woman's but daintier."

"Now the key to surviving the ceremony is remaining quiet," Linnea said, running a brush through my tangled dark hair.

"Surviving?" I echoed. "Is it dangerous?"

"Only if you consider Aunt Hyacinth's wrath dangerous," Aster said.

"Which it is," Linnea added.

"Right, so not literal survival," I said, and breathed a sigh of relief. "It's a shame Marley can't come. She'd get a kick out of the whole thing."

"Next year," Linnea said. "When her magic manifests. There's a special ceremony for new members."

"Isn't that me?" I asked.

Linnea frowned. "Yours is a special case. The new member ceremony is designed for young girls, welcoming them to womanhood."

"So mine is...a fake ceremony?" I asked.

"No, no," Aster assured me. "Nothing like that. An induction is just different. Plus, you're a Rose. Descendants of the One True Witch get special treatment."

No kidding.

"Are you sure I don't need to wear anything under this?" I asked. The white shift dress seemed flimsy for a nighttime outdoor activity.

"It's not too chilly," Aster said. "You should be fine."

"Just wear attractive underpants in case," Linnea said. She hesitated. "You do have attractive underpants, don't you?"

"Depends on your definition of attractive," I replied.

Linnea bit her lip. "You'll be fine."

"Are you sure we don't need shoes?" I asked. "What if we step on a pinecone or something? Those things are sharp."

"Shoes are unnecessary," Linnea insisted.

"How about a dab of gloss and then we'll be all set?" Aster said. She whipped out a tube of pale pink gloss and smeared it across my lips.

"I feel like you're about to marry me off to a sea monster," I said.

"No need to worry about that," Aster said. "The last Kraken was spotted more than fifty years ago. We're pretty sure they've gone extinct."

I swallowed hard. Pretty sure?

A knock on the front door alerted us to Florian's arrival.

"Time to go," Linnea said, with an air of excitement. I guess it wasn't every day they got to have a special ceremony for a new member of the Rose family.

We emerged from the bedroom and went downstairs, where Marley was trying to keep PP3 from growling at Florian.

"He isn't used to having another male around," Marley explained. "He's very protective of us."

"Did he growl like this at your boyfriends?" Florian asked me.

"I wouldn't know," I replied. "I never had any."

He appeared surprised. "Since your husband...You haven't dated anyone?"

I shook my head. "Who has the time?"

Florian grunted. "You sound like Linnea."

"Nothing wrong with sounding like me," Linnea said.

"Have fun, Mom," Marley said, stroking PP3's brown fur. "I guess I'll be asleep when you get home."

Somehow, I doubted that Marley would be able to fall asleep without me here. It was one of the reasons I never went out in the evenings. Her sleep schedule was more important to me than a fun night out.

"Mrs. Babcock is outside," Florian said. "She's brought a batch of homemade cookies and a few games to play."

Mrs. Babcock sounded like a remarkable improvement over me.

"And she's a witch, too?" Marley asked.

"No," Florian said. "She's a brownie."

I laughed. "A brownie that brings cookies."

Marley peered at me. "You don't know what a brownie is, do you?"

I opened my mouth, but no sound came out.

"A brownie is a mythological creature that likes to help around the house," Marley said.

Florian cleared his throat. "Not mythological, I think you'll find. She lives in the attic of the main house."

"Traditionally, brownies only worked the night shift," Linnea said, "but Mrs. Babcock has been with our family for so long, she's willing to come whenever her services are required."

Florian opened the door and called to the brownie. A petite woman entered the room. Her white hair was pulled back in a bun and she wore wire-rimmed glasses and a plain brown dress with loafers.

"You must be Marley," she said, standing nearly at eye level with my daughter. "I've brought treats for us to enjoy while the grown-ups conduct their business."

Marley smiled. "Thank you. I like treats."

Mrs. Babcock winked. "I figured as much." She flicked her hands at us. "Go on now. You don't want to be late for your own ceremony. Things are well in hand here."

I took a final look at Marley before deciding it was okay to leave. To my great relief, she wasn't wearing her usual fearful expression. "See you later."

Outside the cottage, three white horses awaited us.

"I'm sorry," I said, freezing in my tracks. "We're riding *horses*?"

"We can't exactly drive a car into the middle of the forest," Aster said. "Horses are customary."

"These are Bell, Book, and Candle," Florian said. "I'm riding Book."

"Um, I've never ridden a horse before," I said. "Is that a problem?"

"That's why we only have three," Linnea said. "Bell belongs to me. And it seems only appropriate that you and Aster should ride Candle."

"Because my name is Ember," I said, more of a statement than a question.

I watched my cousins mount the horses with ease. I had no clue how to do that. I stood there, staring at the majestic creature. What if I pulled its mane too hard and upset it? What if we went galloping off the edge of the cliff into the ocean, only to discover that Krakens were not, in fact, extinct after all?

I calmed my nerves. Now I understood why Marley was so anxious all the time. It wasn't her intelligence. It was her idiot mother.

"Are you ready, Ember?" Aster asked.

I drew a deep breath. "How do I get up?"

"Oh, of course." She looked thoughtful for a moment. "Let's make it easy, shall we?"

She pointed her finger and made a circular motion. My feet lifted off the ground and I felt my body rise into the air. It was an unsettling feeling.

"Hey," I cried, nervous about falling to the ground. My body was jerked over top of the horse and dropped into the saddle in front of Aster. I felt like one of those claw machines on the boardwalk.

"All comfy?" Aster queried. "Hold on tight."

I gripped the horse's neck as it entered the woods. After a few minutes, my discomfort began to fade. Although it was a bumpy ride, it was fun to see the forest from a different vantage point.

We arrived at a clearing where I spotted at least two dozen people around a circle of large stones. The women wore white dresses like us and the men were dressed in silver cloaks like Florian. I noticed Aunt Hyacinth speaking to a tall woman in a floor-length white dress. A silver crown decorated with a moon sat atop her head and her long silver hair was tied back in a braid that extended to her bottom.

"That's the High Priestess with Mother," Aster whispered as she dismounted. "She'll be performing the ceremony."

I didn't need to ask for help this time. Aster zigzagged a finger and I popped straight off the horse and onto the ground.

A severe-looking man stood beside the High Priestess. Although he wore no crown, he had an air of importance.

"Who's that?" I asked.

"Magnus Destry," Aster whispered. "The High Priest. Don't worry. You'll get a chance to meet people. Everyone is eager to meet you."

"A warm Silver Moon welcome to my lovely niece," Aunt Hyacinth said. I half expected her to be wearing a kaftan and holding a cocktail, even out here in the forest.

"Do they always look so unhappy?" I asked. I observed far more frowns than smiles in the group.

"It's because of the Maiden," Aster said quietly. "The coven is still grappling with her passing."

"Will they talk about her during the ceremony?" I asked. Maybe I'd learn something.

"Definitely not," Aunt Hyacinth said. "Tonight is for you, darling. The Maiden's life was already celebrated in a separate ceremony."

"You weren't invited to attend because you weren't officially a member yet," Aster explained.

"So what happens now?" I asked, surveying the scene.

"As soon as the sun has set, we'll stand around the stone circle and begin the ceremony," Aunt Hyacinth said.

It only took a few minutes for the sun to dip below the horizon. The clearing darkened, and the only light came from the moon and stars above our heads.

"Coven, take your places, please," the High Priestess said. Her voice was warmer than I expected.

Bodies shuffled into position. I stood between Linnea and Aster in front of the stone circle.

"Summoner," the High Priestess said, nodding to a man in a black cloak. He lifted a walking stick and pointed it at the circle until a burst of flames appeared within the stones.

"That's the biggest Aim 'n Flame I've ever seen," I whispered.

"It's a blackthorn staff," Linnea whispered.

Whatever. As far as I was concerned, it was a giant, wooden Aim 'n Flame. I could use one of those for my new fireplace.

"What's a Summoner?" I asked.

"The understudy to the High Priest," Linnea answered quietly.

"O' wondrous Goddess of the Moon," the High Priestess began. "We ask that you join us in welcoming a long-absent member of the coven. We are grateful to have Yarrow Rose walk among us once again. We thank you for your generous bounty."

I cringed at the mention of my birth name. "Ember," I hissed.

"Thank you, Goddess of the Moon," everyone chanted. The wind picked up and I gripped the bottom half of my dress.

The High Priestess produced a silver wand and dipped the end into the flames. She came toward me, smiling warmly. It was only after she stood directly in front of me that I realized she walked *straight through the stone circle.* Popcorn balls of fire! Her dress wasn't even singed. How did she do that?

"Yarrow Rose, we welcome you to the bosom of the Silver Moon coven. You have our allegiance and our protection." She touched the tip of her wand to my forehead and drew some kind of design. I resisted the urge to cross my eyes and look.

"We are honor bound to teach you the ways of the coven and to assist you in managing your magic responsibly."

Well, that was just smart business. The coven didn't want me running around using magic willy-nilly and giving them a bad name. I was bound to destroy something. I'd be like magical Godzilla, knocking down buildings and leveling whole towns. Except mine would be accidental. I was pretty sure Godzilla's moves were deliberate, though it had been years since I'd watched any of the films.

The High Priestess returned to her position in the circle. I noticed a stout woman to my left, busily typing away on her iPhone. Talk about inappropriate texting.

"What on earth?" I asked in a harsh whisper, elbowing Aster. She followed my judgmental gaze.

Aster resisted the urge to smile. "That's Gardenia, the coven Scribe. Don't worry. She's only taking notes on her phone. She keeps minutes of the meetings and handles correspondence."

Oh. Judgment withdrawn.

The High Priestess held her arms up high and began to chant in a language I didn't understand. The rest of the coven followed suit. I stood there, feeling like a cheerleader who didn't learn the routine before the big game.

The man in black retrieved his giant Aim 'n Flame again

and pointed it at the glowing fire. "Extinguish," he said, and the flames quickly melted away.

Everyone clapped. Aster and Linnea hugged me.

"Come on," Aster said. "Let's introduce you to everyone."

Someone handed me a cup filled with steaming liquid. Not a cocktail then. Darn. I brought the drink to my lips and tasted it. Some type of apple cider. I swallowed. Ooh. It had a pleasant kick after all.

Linnea dragged me in front of an old woman with white hair and rounded shoulders. Clearly, no one had warned her about osteoporosis when she was younger.

"Ember, I'd like you to meet Calla," Linnea said. "She's the Crone."

I jerked my chin toward Linnea. "That's not very polite." Not that I was one to talk. I was already having harsh thoughts about the woman's insufficient milk drinking.

"It's not an insult," Linnea said. "The Crone is a coveted title within the coven. Calla was a former High Priestess. She's quite skilled in herbalism and magic."

Calla sounded like a useful member of the coven. Unlike me.

"And I am the Mother," another woman said, stepping forward. She looked around forty with high cheekbones and strawberry blond waves that cascaded down her shoulders.

"Zahara," Linnea said. "Explain the role of the Mother to my cousin."

"I'm responsible for coordinating rituals and overseeing coven projects and activities. I arranged tonight's ceremony, for example."

"Oh, thanks," I said. "It's nothing like I expected. Very cool in the dark with the moon and everything."

"Yes, most of our rituals take place under a canopy of stars," Zahara said. "Our magic is drawn from Nature's energy so it seems appropriate."

"Really? That's the source of the magic?" I asked.

"For our coven, yes," Zahara replied. "Not all covens are the same, mind you. Magic manifests differently in different witches."

"I wish I knew more about mine," I said. "I can make it rain. That's about the extent of my knowledge so far."

Zahara gave me a sympathetic smile. "It's my understanding that you'll be meeting with the Mistress-of-Runecraft. The first step in your magical education."

Runecraft sounded like a video game. "Why does everyone else seem to know my schedule better than I do?"

Zahara lowered her voice. "Welcome to the family of Hyacinth Rose-Muldoon."

Aster came over to steer me away. "There are other people over here who'd like to meet you..." She didn't finish her statement.

The pounding of footsteps caused everyone to freeze in place. A howl pierced the momentary silence, causing the hair on the back of my neck to stand on end. Just because I knew there were werewolves here didn't mean I was okay with seeing one. Or a dozen.

Witches and wizards screamed in protest as a pack of wolves tore through the clearing, trampling the carefully laid stone circle.

"Wyatt Nash, you know perfectly well we're having a ceremony here tonight," Linnea yelled, and stomped her foot for good measure. She turned to her sister. "He overheard me telling the kids before I went out. He came by to fix one of the gutters."

One of the wolves trotted over to Linnea and—sweet baby Elvis—a naked man stood right where the wolf had been. I clamped a hand over my mouth. No one else seemed remotely bothered by the man's nudity.

"It's a full moon, Linnea," the wolf-turned-man said. "This is our turf during the full moon."

Gardenia, the stout Scribe, waddled over, waving her phone in the air. "I have a record of the permit right here, Wyatt. The coven was granted permission to use this space tonight after sundown."

Wyatt barely glanced at the screen. His gaze was pinned on Linnea. "You look pretty in that white dress. Reminds me of our wedding." He wiggled his eyebrows. "And our wedding night."

Linnea shook her fist. "Get out of here, Wyatt, and take your filthy pups with you."

Some of the wolves growled in response and Wyatt quieted them with a fierce look.

"Apologies for the interruption, everyone," Wyatt said, and bowed with a flourish before shifting back into a wolf and rejoining the pack. They ran off through the woods, howling.

"Okay," I said, the image of Wyatt Nash's bare butt burned into my brain. "*Now* it's nothing like I expected."

CHAPTER 10

"MOM, THIS LIBRARY IS AMAZING," Marley said. Her voice was so loud that I waited for a librarian to shush us.

"I'm glad you approve," I said.

Marley had insisted that her after-school activity involve a visit to the town library. She'd been disappointed by the offerings at the middle school library and wanted a larger selection. Same old Marley.

She dragged me by the hand to the desk. There were two women behind the counter, hunched over a screen. They seemed to be debating something. The auburn-haired woman glanced up to greet us.

"Welcome to the Starry Hollow library," she said. "How can I help you today?"

Marley eagerly stepped up to the counter. "We'd like library cards, please."

The woman smiled down at her. "Of course. We're always happy to welcome new members. I just need to see your passports."

Marley and I exchanged uneasy glances. Oops. We still didn't have passports.

"We're new in town," I said. "Apparently, we need to jump through some hoops to get passports, and we haven't managed to do that yet." According to Linnea, we had to wait for the Council of Elders to meet and two of them were away on vacation.

The woman frowned. "I'm sorry. I can't do anything for you without ID."

I hesitated to invoke my aunt's name. I didn't want to be one of those people who threw her weight around town. I had no experience with being a 'Have' versus a 'Have Not.'

Marley stepped closer to the counter. "My name is Marley Rose, and my great-aunt is Hyacinth Rose-Muldoon," she said in her most authoritative voice. "Perhaps you've heard of her."

My head snapped to attention. *Marley* was playing the Rose-Muldoon card? Man, she really wanted that library card.

The woman's eyes widened slightly. "Of course. I've heard all about your arrival. My name is Delphine Winter, and I'm also a member of the Silver Moon coven."

Marley smiled. "You're a witch, too?" Her voice dropped to a soft whisper.

Delphine leaned down. "I am. And you can tell whomever you like. Paranormals live completely open lives in Starry Hollow."

"Yeah, we noticed," I said.

Delphine smiled at me. "It's a pleasure to meet you both. I'm sorry I missed the ceremony, but I'm sure we'll be seeing each other often."

Marley brightened. "Does this mean we can have library cards?"

"I'd be happy to prepare cards for you." Delphine set to work entering data into the computer. "Sorry, I'll just be a moment. My assistant and I have been trying to clean up some records. We have several books missing with no record of being checked out. These things happen on occasion."

"You mean like *Fifty Shades of Grey?*" I joked. Maybe paranormal readers were just like human ones and didn't want anyone to know which types of books they preferred to read.

Delphine's brow furrowed. "I haven't heard of that one. No, a random assortment of titles has disappeared. No rhyme or reason that we can tell." She scanned the list on the screen. "*My Sorceress, Myself, Successful Vampire Transitions, Full Moon Over Miami,* and *Are You There, Mother Nature? It's Me, the Adolescent Witch.* It's a drain on our resources to hunt them down."

"At least people here seem to like to read," Marley said. "An investment in knowledge pays the best interest."

Delphine broke into a wide smile. "A Benjamin Franklin fan, are you? Some coven members are convinced he had access to magic. Well, I'm very excited to welcome you to the library, young lady. You'll make a fine addition to Starry Hollow."

Marley beamed like someone had just given her the key to the city.

"You should really get those passports taken care of as soon as possible," Delphine said. "If you're new in town, you're going to need ID for many purposes. Starry Hollow likes its bureaucracy almost as much as it likes its magic."

She finished typing on the keyboard and I heard the whirring sound of a printer.

"Let me get these laminated for you and you'll be all set," Delphine said.

"Can I check out a book today?" Marley asked.

"You may as well go look now," Delphine said. "By the time your card is ready, I expect you'll have found something to borrow."

"Do you know where I can find books about witches and their familiars?" Marley asked.

Ah, the cat obsession was intensifying.

"If you stand in that section over there"—Delphine pointed to the far right of the library—"and say a few keywords like 'witch' and 'familiar,' a selection of books will glide over to you."

Marley's eyes sparkled. "Glide over to me?"

Delphine nodded. "That's right. No more reading spines with your head cocked to the side. You simply announce the type of book you're looking for and magic should help you find what you're looking for."

I didn't even have a chance to say anything before Marley skipped away and disappeared into the stacks of books.

"I was told I could find you here."

I whipped around. "Florian?"

He glanced around the library like he'd never seen it before. "It's nice in here."

Delphine nervously brushed the hair out of her eyes. "Good afternoon, Florian."

"How did you know I was here?" I asked. "Did one of you tag me with a tracking device?" I wouldn't put it past Aunt Hyacinth.

"It's called magic," Florian said. "A simple locator spell using a piece of hair from your brush."

I squinted. "You were in the cottage?"

"Mother sent Simon to fetch it." He chuckled. "Simon gets all the sophisticated jobs."

"So what's the emergency?" I asked. "Marley is checking out a few books."

"Mother has arranged for you to start your job this afternoon," Florian said. "I'm tasked with giving you the details. Mother likes to keep me occupied, you see."

I glanced at the clock on the wall. "Now?" I shook my

head, trying to process. "What job? Why has no one discussed this with me?"

Florian clapped me on the shoulder. "Welcome to Mother's world. The rest of us just drink in it."

"Okay, where am I going?"

"*Vox Populi*," he said.

"It sounds like you've named a disease. What is that?"

"A weekly newspaper. Mother owns it."

Ah. "I don't really have administrative skills," I said. "I type at my own pace and I'm terrible on the phone. I have this bad habit of hanging up on callers that annoy me."

"Good thing you won't be an assistant then," he replied. "She's instructed the editor to offer you a place as a reporter."

I laughed in his face. "I'm not qualified to be a reporter."

"You need a job, don't you?" Florian queried.

"Yes, but something more...me."

He rested his elbow on the counter. "What's more you?"

"I don't know." I struggled to come up with a suggestion. "Do paranormals have their cars repossessed or is that a human thing?"

His blue eyes softened. "Ember, you're being given the chance to climb out of the hole you managed to dig for yourself and your daughter. Don't waste it."

"Hole? Well, that's just insulting."

Florian sniffed. "Go to the newspaper office, cousin. I'll take Marley back to the cottage."

"Fine," I huffed, and pointed a finger at him. "But you tell that Simon to keep out of my underwear drawer."

He made a symbol with his fingers. "Wizard's honor."

The newspaper office was located right on Coastline Drive. Although my experience in newspaper offices was nonexistent, this seemed like a pretty nice one. Any place with an ocean view was luxurious as far as I was concerned. The office was what I would call Goldilocks-sized, not too big and not too small. Six desks filled the room, as well as two private offices with closed doors in the back.

A woman fluttered over to me, her green wings glistening in the afternoon sunlight that streamed through the front windows. Her smile was nearly as bright as the sparkle of her wings.

"You must be Ember Rose," the fairy said, pumping my hand. "My name is Tanya and I'm the office manager here. I keep everything ticking along nicely."

"Good to meet you, Tanya," I said. I wasn't convinced I would ever get used to seeing people with wings on a day that wasn't Halloween.

She gestured to the room. "Why don't you follow me and I'll introduce you to the associate editor?" She fluttered toward the closest desk, where a young man was in the middle of a phone conversation.

"No, completely off the record," he said. "You know me, Larry. My word is as good as a blood oath. Garland, did you say?" He typed notes into his phone at lightning speed. "She was her herbology partner? Well, that's useful, since she died from hemlock." He glanced up and saw me standing there. "Listen, I gotta run, but thanks for this. I'll be in touch." He hung up the phone and smiled. "I've got a lead about the dead Maiden."

"Are you covering the murder?" I asked.

He nodded. "It's a big story in town. Prominent young girl with a bright future." He scanned me. "And then there's you. A legacy hire. I haven't seen one of you since Florian got a job here."

"Wait. Florian works here?" I queried. Why didn't he mention that?

"Not anymore," the editor said. "So obviously you can see how that worked out. I imagine you'll be much the same."

I took an instant dislike to him. "Aunt Hyacinth knows I have absolutely no experience. I'm not trying to fool anybody."

"Good thing," he said. "Because you'd have to die trying around here. We don't suffer fools gladly in this office." He stood to shake my hand. "I'm Bentley Smith, by the way."

"So are you my new boss?" I asked.

He grinned. "You're the FNG. We're all your new bosses, even Tanya."

Tanya gave me a sympathetic look. "Bentley is yanking your wings," she said. "There's only one boss around here and that's Mr. Hale."

"I thought it was Aunt Hyacinth. Isn't she the owner?"

Tanya cringed. "Yes, of course. Her, too."

At that moment, the door to one of the back offices swung open and a man appeared in the doorway. He wore a crisp, cream-colored linen suit and a pale blue tie. He looked like he belonged on the cover of a men's fashion magazine. His golden blond hair was slicked back, amplifying his chiseled jaw and piercing green eyes.

My pulse began to race. Oh, my. Come to mama.

"Mr. Hale, impeccable timing as always," Tanya said. "I'd like you to see me about..."

Mr. Hale crossed the room with surprising grace for a man of his six-foot-two-inch stature.

"Interesting," he said, inspecting me. "I don't see the family resemblance. The Rose genes are usually so...apparent."

I couldn't decide whether that was an insult. "I take after my mother, or so I'm told."

Mr. Hale's mouth twitched. "We shall see about that."

What did that mean? "So I understand you're my new

boss." I stuck out my hand. "I have no idea what I'm doing, but I'll do my best at whatever it is."

He glanced quickly at my hand before accepting it. Was he looking for germs? Because I was pretty sure those were not visible to the naked eye. Unless he was some kind of magical creature that could see molecules and crap like that. Did a creature like that even exist?

"I'm a vampire," he said, as though answering my unasked question. "And you should learn to shield your thoughts around us."

My mouth dropped open. "Wait. You're a psychic vampire? That's a thing?"

"We cannot read minds in the way that you imagine," he replied. "But if the thinker is open enough, we are able to glean flashes of information. It certainly helps in the information-gathering business."

No doubt. "I hate to ask, but how exactly do I go about shielding my thoughts?" Because I was having a hell of a lot of thoughts right now and I didn't want Mr. Hale to get flashes of any of them.

"I suspect you should speak to your aunt about that. The coven is very adept at providing such tutelage."

A sharp dresser and fifty-cent words. Mr. Hale was not going to be my typical boss. Hilda generally came to the office in sweatpants and a tank top in the summer, and a spare deodorant in the drawer. She wasn't concerned with appearances, as long as she got results.

"So what exactly will I be reporting on?" I asked.

Bentley's hyena laugh was cut short by a sharp look from Mr. Hale.

"We thought you could start with school sports," Mr. Hale said. "Citizens always like reading about their children's achievements."

"Does it matter that I don't know anything about sports?"

"Really?" His brow raised a fraction. "Nothing at all? How unusual for a human."

"My husband was a football fan," I said. "I never got into it myself. Too violent with all of that sacking and whatever else they do."

Mr. Hale observed me coolly. "Violent? American football?" He clucked his tongue. "Miss Rose, you and I have very different views on what constitutes violence."

"Violence is in the eye of the beholder, I guess," I said.

"I do believe that is beauty," he said. *And you certainly have that in spades.*

I blinked. I swore he just complimented me, but I didn't see his mouth move. How was that possible? I thought *he* was the psychic. Now I was psychic, too? I pressed my fingers to my temples.

"Is something wrong?" Tanya asked.

"No, sorry. I suddenly felt lightheaded," I said.

"I'll fetch you a glass of water," she said, in an attempt to mother me. "Do sit down, Miss Rose."

"Call me Ember," I said.

"Ember," Mr. Hale said. "Such an unusual name for a witch."

I forced a smile. "I found out recently that I was called Yarrow when I was born. I'm glad that name never gained a foothold." I didn't get into the fact that my father changed my name when he left Starry Hollow. Mr. Hale didn't need all the sordid details of my past.

"Welcome to the staff," Mr. Hale said. "Now, if you'll excuse me, I have an appointment elsewhere."

"It was nice to meet you...um," I said. "What should I call you?"

He frowned at me. "I'm not sure I catch your meaning."

"I'm Ember," I said. "What do I call you?"

He inclined his head. "Mr. Hale, of course."

He strode out the front door without a backward glance.

Bentley burst into laughter. "Boy, you've got a lot to learn." He rubbed his hands together. "You're going to provide endless entertainment, if nothing else."

Bentley was suddenly becoming the brother I never wanted. Tanya handed me a glass of water and I drank it greedily. I hadn't realized how thirsty I was until I felt the cool liquid slide down my throat.

"Salty air will do that to you," Tanya said.

I nodded, swallowing. "It will definitely take some getting used to, but I like it."

"I do recommend learning some shielding techniques," Tanya said, lowering her voice. I wasn't sure why she bothered, since Mr. Hale was no longer in the building. "If he wants to extract information, it's difficult to stop him. On a normal day, though, it's best to have your defenses up. You never know when you might think something inappropriate. Goodness knows how many times I've grumbled in my head about working overtime and thanked the gods he didn't hear me."

Definitely good to know.

"Did you know that I'm on the sheriff's list of suspects?" I asked. "He interviewed me because I found the body."

Bentley looked interested. "You've suddenly become useful, Rose. Tell me everything."

I made myself comfortable and launched into the story.

CHAPTER 11

"WE'RE READY FOR YOU, EMBER," my aunt's voice called.

The two missing members of the Council of Elders had finally returned from their vacation, so the process for obtaining passport approval was fast-tracked by one of the key council members—you guessed it—Aunt Hyacinth.

The Council of Elders didn't meet in a town hall like I expected. Instead, they met in a cave located on a secluded beach on the edge of town, not far from Fairy Cove. My aunt had escorted me there on horseback. For a woman partial to silver platters and a driver, she rode a horse like nobody's business.

I entered the cave and was surprised by how light and airy it was. I ran a hand along a stone wall until I reached an even larger opening. An enormous round table sat in the middle of the room surrounded by paranormals in cloaks.

"Come and sit next to me," Aunt Hyacinth called, gesturing me over.

"That's only if she doesn't have anything nice to say," a man joked. Based on his tiny stature and slightly green skin, I was betting on a leprechaun.

Aunt Hyacinth shot him a dirty look. "Control yourself, Mervin O'Malley. Save your jokes for comedy night at the Pot of Gold. This is my niece and I'll not be disrespected in front of her."

Mervin sank lower in his chair, which made it difficult to see his face.

I settled in beside my aunt and tried not to feel intimidated by the seven cloaks around the table. I noticed that each cloak was a different color—red, green, brown, black, blue, and yellow. My aunt's cloak was silver, cinched together by a lapel pin of a red rose.

I squirmed in my seat. This was worse than the time I got called to the principal's office for smoking in the girls' bathroom. I'd only been holding Caitlin Anton's cigarette while she flushed. I swear. No, the principal didn't believe me either.

"So is this a normal Tuesday night for you guys?" I asked. "No poker?"

"Poker is Thursdays," the man in the brown cloak said. Based on the multiple hair violations, including the length of his nose hairs, my money was on werewolf.

"Arthur Rutledge, she was making a joke," Aunt Hyacinth said. "My niece seems to have a particular brand of humor."

I gave her a serious case of side-eye. 'Particular' did *not* sound like a compliment.

"Let's get started, shall we? Now that we've established your lineage and you've been welcomed by the coven," Aunt Hyacinth said, "it's time to make it official and sort out your paperwork."

"That involves a little Q&A session," Mervin said. "We like to get to know our new residents. Make sure they're a good fit for the community."

"Like an immigration interview?" I queried.

"I suppose," Aunt Hyacinth said. "We do reserve the right

to reject people." She placed a hand over mine. "But not you, dear. Not to worry. You are a Rose, after all."

I caught the discreet roll of Arthur's eyes. Apparently, my aunt used this line a lot.

I placed my hands on the table, palms down. "So what kinds of questions do you have for me? Height? Weight? Place of birth?" I laughed. "Oh, wait. Place of birth was here."

"Where have you been living since you left Starry Hollow?" the woman in the yellow cloak asked. "I'm Misty Brookline, by the way." She shrugged off her cloak for a moment and her wings sparkled in the dim light of the cave. "Fairy."

I nodded. "I'm from Maple Shade, New Jersey. My father raised me on his own."

"He never remarried?" the woman in the black cloak asked. Her pale skin was offset by thick, mahogany-colored hair. When she spoke, I detected a set of fangs.

"This is Victorine Del Bianco," Aunt Hyacinth said. "She's the leader of the vampires in this town."

"No, Ms. Del Bianco," I replied, feeling a lump in my throat. "He was devoted to my mother. He never got over her death."

"And you have a child, we understand," Victorine said.

"A ten-year-old daughter called Marley. She's amazing."

"And your husband is deceased?" the elderly woman in the red cloak asked. With her heavily wrinkled skin and flabby arms, she appeared more of a crone than the Crone. I guess that's why she served on the Council of Elders.

"Amaryllis Elderflower, I already told you he was dead," Aunt Hyacinth said sharply. "Don't belabor the point. My niece has suffered enough in her short life."

"That's okay," I said. "I don't mind answering. He died four years ago in an accident."

"What was his name, dear?" Amaryllis asked.

"Karl," I replied. "Karl Holmes."

The man in the blue cloak held up a finger to speak. "Oliver Dagwood here, former High Priest of the coven. I'd like to know where you met this Karl Holmes. Was he a paranormal?"

"No, at least not that I know of." To be fair, I didn't know *I* was a paranormal until recently. "We met in high school, in ninth grade, but didn't start dating until the end of tenth grade."

"Spell's bells, you were just children," Amaryllis said.

"Yeah, we were," I agreed. But we'd been fairly happy. Not puppies and rainbows happy, but still...who was?

"Tell us about where you've been living," Arthur said, leaning forward. "Were you really being pursued by the mob?"

I shot a quizzical look at my aunt. Was she revealing all my secrets to the council?

"I had a run-in with a member of a New Jersey crime family," I said carefully.

"New Jersey, New York. I love that whole area. Full of such characters," Mervin said, with a laugh that sounded more like a hiccup. "Did he tell you he wouldn't fuggedabout you?"

"Let me think. First, he set fire to the truck I was in, and then he came to my apartment and tried to burn down the building with everyone in it." I tapped my chin thoughtfully. "So, yeah, I guess it's safe to say he wasn't going to fuggedabout me."

"Is it true there are a lot of diners in New Jersey?" Amaryllis asked. "I love a good diner omelet with a side of hash browns." She rubbed her stomach.

"Um, yeah. I guess. Marley and I liked to eat at a place called the Olive Branch Diner." Pancakes for dinner was always a treat for both of us. Marley liked to get whipped cream on hers.

"I bet you're a crazy driver," Arthur said. "Maybe we shouldn't give her a driver's license here."

"Hey," I objected. "I'm an excellent driver. If anything, driving in New Jersey qualifies me to drive anywhere in the world." Including Italy.

"She has a point, Arthur," Amaryllis said.

"What about this business with the sheriff?" Arthur inquired. "I heard from Granger Nash that you were questioned about Fleur Montbatten's death."

"That's because Sheriff Nash would love any opportunity to drag the good Rose name through the proverbial mud," Aunt Hyacinth said with a sniff.

I shrugged. "I found the body, so the sheriff said I'm a suspect until he finds evidence to the contrary."

Arthur's eyebrows knitted together. "I see."

"My niece will get all the paperwork she requires and no one here will say boo about it," Aunt Hyacinth said. She glanced around the table, daring anyone to speak.

Arthur heaved a sigh. "I'm sorry, Hyacinth, but I think until your niece's name has been officially cleared, we can't possibly approve a passport for her. And her daughter's passport is dependent on the legal adult's."

I could tell from my aunt's hardened expression that Arthur was going to wake up tomorrow with a snake in place of a body part.

"Arthur has a point," Misty said.

"Of course he does," Aunt Hyacinth snapped. "Arthur always has a point where you're concerned, Misty. Allow me to let you in on a little secret. That ship has sailed. No amount of licking his paws will get you back into his...good graces."

Misty's cheeks burned. "If we make an exception for your niece, we could set a bad precedent."

Aunt Hyacinth composed herself. "Very well then. If the vote isn't unanimous, then we'll table the issue of the passports until the investigation has been concluded and my niece's good name has been cleared."

"If we're almost finished, I have a question," I said, raising my hand.

"Miss Rose, there's no need to raise your hand," Victorine said. "This isn't school."

A group of judging eyes surrounding you? Interrogating you? It sure felt like it.

"Why does no one here say *y'all?*" I asked. "I thought everyone in the South said *y'all.*"

"That's your question?" Victorine pursed her lips, clearly disappointed.

"I'm sure I'll have more," I said, "but that's the first one that sprang to mind."

"While we are geographically located in the South, we exist in our own magical bubble, if you will," Victorine replied.

"But people can come and go," I said. "They're not trapped in the bubble."

"Oh no," Victorine said. "We're not like Spellbound. As you saw when you arrived in Starry Hollow, access is easy, albeit closely monitored."

"What's Spellbound?" I asked.

"An unfortunate incident in Pennsylvania," Aunt Hyacinth said. "A cursed town where the paranormals can't enter or exit."

"They brought it upon themselves," Amaryllis grumbled.

"We don't know that," Victorine snapped.

Aunt Hyacinth banged her fist on the table. "That's

enough, councilors." She swiveled her head toward me. "Any more questions, Ember?"

"Who's going to teach me how to use my magic? And how can I shield my thoughts from a vampire?" I looked quickly at Victorine. "No offense."

"Yes, there is the issue of your education," Aunt Hyacinth said. "We thought it would be best if the coven took you on as a group project."

"A group project?" I echoed.

"Yes, we'll have each specialist work with you individually, beginning with the Mistress-of-Runecraft."

"The mistress of what now?" The odd name sounded familiar. I was sure someone had mentioned it before.

Aunt Hyacinth patted my hand. "I'll explain later, dear. Just know that your education will be taken seriously."

"Because I'm a Rose, after all?" I queried.

She winked. "Now you're catching on."

CHAPTER 12

STARRY HOLLOW HIGH SCHOOL looked like any other typical American high school. I was mildly disappointed that it wasn't a Hogwarts-style castle, even though I knew it would be unlikely in a Southern seaside town.

At two-thirty on the dot, the double doors burst open and hundreds of hormones came tumbling out. It struck me that in three short years, I'd have a teenager of my own. It hardly seemed possible. Would she start dressing like some of these girls, with their short skirts and overdone makeup? Unlikely. Marley wasn't a typical ten-year-old, so I highly doubted she'd become a typical teenager.

I grabbed the nearest boy. He looked about fourteen with acne dotting his cheeks. "Do you know a girl called Garland?"

The boy looked at me like I was nuts. Maybe I was. "Of course I know Garland. Everyone knows everyone in this town."

"Can you point her out for me? I need to speak with her." After the council's passport rejection, I'd decided to take matters into my own hands and clear my name. I remembered Bentley's phone call that mentioned Garland as Fleur's herbology partner. May as well start with her.

The boy stepped away from the crowd to better observe the students still exiting the building. His expression lit up and he pointed. "There she is. Brown hair and glasses."

I saw her immediately. She reminded me of Velma from Scooby Doo and I suppressed the urge to laugh. All she needed was an orange turtleneck sweater and a 'jinkies' catchphrase.

"Thanks, kid," I said.

"My name's Scott."

"Yeah, okay. Whatever."

He gave me a disapproving look. "That isn't very polite, Miss Rose."

I stopped walking and turned to face him. "You know who I am?"

He nodded. "I told you. Everyone knows everyone in this town." He gave me a small smile. "Don't worry. You'll get used to it."

I doubted that very much. I was used to living an anonymous life. I could count on one hand the number of neighbors I knew in my apartment building.

I made a beeline for Garland before she could disappear down the block. "Garland, excuse me," I called.

Garland halted and turned around, a large book clutched to her chest. It looked like it hadn't been dusted in years. You would think they could afford a decent janitor in a town as nice as this one.

"I'm Garland," she said, scrutinizing me. "You're the long-lost Rose woman, aren't you? Can I help you find something?"

"Is there somewhere we can talk for a few minutes in private?"

Garland glanced around, thinking. "The greenhouse will be empty this time of day. I'll take you there."

What a surprise that the herbology student wanted to meet in the greenhouse. It was appropriate, if nothing else.

I followed her across school grounds to an enormous greenhouse. I was expecting something that you'd find in a backyard. A small and manageable greenhouse. This one was the size of an Olympic pool. We stepped inside and I immediately felt transported to a magical plant kingdom.

"It's incredible in here," I said. Color jumped out at me from every angle and the smells were intoxicating.

Garland smiled. "It *is* pretty special, isn't it? Do you like plants?"

"Probably not since I've killed every plant I've ever owned." And that included a cactus, allegedly one of the hardest to kill.

"That doesn't mean you dislike them," Garland said. "It just means you're inept at caring for them."

Way to rub it in, Captain Obvious. "I don't recognize a lot of these flowers."

"There's a mixture of plants, herbs, and flowers in here. The students use them for potions and spells. They wouldn't all be available in the human world."

"Potions and spells? The closest I came to any class like that was chemistry," I said.

"Mixology and herbology have a lot in common with chemistry. I spend a lot of time in here," Garland said. "Some people have comfort food. I have a comfort space." She touched the leaves of a nearby tree. "Whenever I feel like I don't belong, I come in here and sit for a while. I always feel better when I leave."

Typical teenager. Feeling like she didn't fit in. I didn't know a person alive who didn't have that feeling at one time or another.

"So plants are your thing, huh?"

Garland nodded and pushed her glasses back up her nose. "I want that to be my specialty when I'm older. My teachers say I'm a natural."

"And you were partners with Fleur in your herbology class. Is that right?"

Garland gave me a funny look. "Is that what this is about? Do you have questions about her?"

"I do." Did you kill her because she was the Daphne to your Velma? "I'm trying to talk to anyone who spent time with her."

"Is this because you're a suspect?" she asked, inclining her head. "You're the one who found her, right? If rumors are to be believed."

Boy, gossip really did get around town quickly. "No, no. I'm working for *Vox Populi*, my family's newspaper. They want me to write a piece on her since I'm a new witch. They think it will be educational for me." Lies and more lies.

"What do you think I would say about her?" Garland asked. "She was the Maiden, after all. That meant she was pretty special."

I eyed her closely. "Did that bother you? That she was chosen to be the Maiden?"

Garland shrugged. "I think it always hurts when someone is chosen over you for something. It doesn't really matter whether you actually wanted it."

"So are you saying you didn't want to be the Maiden?"

"I liked the idea of being special, of course, but the Maiden is a big responsibility." Garland surveyed the greenhouse. "And I already have my passion in life. If I were the Maiden, I'd need to focus on *her* responsibilities. That would mean sacrificing my own."

Wow. A passion at sixteen years old. My passion at sixteen was admiring how good my butt looked in jeans.

Garland didn't know how lucky she was. Some people spent their whole lives never figuring out where their true passions lie. Hell, I was one of them.

"What about Fleur? Was she sacrificing a passion that you know of?"

Garland laughed. "If you count non-coven friends as a passion, then yes. She spent most of her time with other paranormals like Uri, like she was too good for witches. Made me question their decision to appoint her as the Maiden."

"Who's Uri?"

"A vampire in our class. There's a group that hangs out together, not that I ever get included."

"How would you describe Fleur's relationship with Uri?"

Garland tended to a potted plant. "Best friends. I felt sorry for them."

"Sorry because they were best friends? Why?"

"Because she was the Maiden and Uri's a hot vampire. She'd never know whether their relationship could have been more."

"Maybe that's what kept their relationship strong," I said. "The forbidden nature of it."

"The friendship itself wasn't forbidden. It was the understanding that there was no possibility of more. They had such nice chemistry." She sighed. "I think they would have made a perfect couple."

"Did she even want a romantic relationship with him? Maybe she was perfectly content with the friendship." I'd had plenty of male friends growing up without any desire for more.

Garland snorted. "No clue. We didn't exactly confide in each other. I'm giving you my own observations."

Garland did seem observant. Then again, outsiders usually were. "Where would be a good place to find Uri?"

Garland took out her wand and tapped it against a few of the hanging plants. "He's in an art class today that meets on Balefire Beach at sunset. He and Fleur were taking the class together."

"Thanks." I paused. "Um, out of curiosity, did you just use a magic wand to water those plants?"

She blinked. "Of course. How else would I do it?"

Okay then.

"So how was Fleur as an herbology partner? Any friction between the two of you?"

Garland sighed. "Only because she didn't hold her weight. I was doing the minotaur's share of the work. She would show up and do the bare minimum and we'd get the same credit."

"I bet you didn't like that very much."

She pushed up her glasses again. "Who would? Everyone likes to feel appreciated. Fleur didn't even acknowledge that I was doing most of the work. She seemed to take it for granted. Typical popular girl attitude."

Resentment rolled off Garland in waves. "Did it make you angry?"

Garland snapped a stem in half. "Of course it did. It wasn't fair. She got to have everything. The title of Maiden, a great group of friends, the good looks, and the grades for things she didn't do."

"What are you doing?" I asked, nodding toward the stem.

She glanced absently at the flower on the floor in front of her. "It's called deadheading."

That sounded violent.

"What do you know about hemlock?" I asked.

Her expression brightened. "That's one of my specialties. I want to be the coven's foremost expert in fatal plants and flowers."

So she openly admitted that hemlock was one of her

specialties. Garland was either a fool or completely innocent, and she certainly didn't strike me as a fool.

"You do realize that Fleur died from hemlock?"

Garland's face fell. "I hadn't heard that. How is that possible? It's really difficult to get access to hemlock."

"I think that's a question the sheriff might be asking you soon," I said. "I guess you have access to hemlock because, as you say, it's one of your specialties."

Garland looked stricken. "Am I a suspect? I have no idea how hemlock would've gotten into her system. I'm very careful with it."

Although I felt a little guilty for frightening her, I wanted to gauge her reaction. I didn't have a lot of transferable skills, but detecting a lie was certainly one of them.

"Did you and Fleur work with hemlock together at any point?"

Garland nodded emphatically. "Yes, recently. It was part of our herbology project. We even needed special permission to use it because normally deadly plants aren't permitted."

"Was it one of those projects where you did most of the work?"

"Of course. She was too busy hanging out with her friends and shadowing the High Priestess to help me with any of it."

"Is there anyone else who might've had access to hemlock during this time?"

Garland heaved a regretful sigh. "No, we were the only ones. That doesn't look good for me, does it?"

Although I agreed that it didn't look good for her, she passed my sniff test. Garland clearly had her own path in life, and it wasn't the same as Fleur's. Garland's jealousy didn't seem to rise to a murderous level, just an annoyed one.

"Okay, one last question," I said.

"What's that?"

"Do you have any clue what time the soccer game is? I'm supposed to cover it for the paper and I have no clue when or where it is."

Garland squinted at me behind her glasses. "Games are usually at five on the field behind the school."

"Perfect. Thanks."

"Mom, why do I need to be here?" Marley complained. "Can't I just go back to the cottage and read?"

"You have to be here," I said. "You know more about soccer than I do."

"That's not saying much," Marley said. "I've never actually played soccer. I've just heard other kids talking about it."

"That's more exposure than I've had," I said.

We stared at the field together. It looked like a bunch of kids running around willy-nilly. Oh wait, there was a ball, too.

"I wish you had to cover Quidditch instead," Marley said.

"I don't know if they play any magical sports here," I said. "I guess since this is a mixed school, not everyone has magical abilities."

"That's true," she said. "You should ask if you'll be covering any sports for the Black Cloak Academy. I bet they do magical sports. I'd go to watch those."

I glanced down at her. "Marley Rose, are you suggesting that you might be interested in playing a sport next year if it's magical?"

She shrugged. "I think I might be tempted."

Hallelujah. Anything to get that girl's nose out of a book and into the real world for a change.

"I think a team just scored," Marley said.

"Popcorn balls," I said. "Which one?"

"The red one," Marley replied.

I tried to remember which team was the red one. I'd have to take notes. There was no way I'd remember all the details to type up later.

As I watched the game unfold, a striking figure in a navy blue suit caught my attention. Mr. Hale crossed the field looking every bit as dapper as the day I'd met him in the office. I was pretty certain he was checking up on me. At least that's what I'd do.

"Hey there, boss," I said, when he reached us.

"Miss Rose," he said, nodding crisply. His focus shifted to Marley. "And who might this be?"

"My daughter, Marley," I said. "Marley, this is my boss, Mr. Hale."

Marley offered her hand. "Nice to meet you, Mr. Hale. I loved your article on the ethical issues surrounding synthetic blood. It's a brave, new world, isn't it? We still have so much to learn."

His expression softened. "We certainly do. Between you and me, I'm following up with a source on possible contamination of one of the largest synthetic blood companies in the country. Bloodspring happens to be based here in Starry Hollow."

"Cool," Marley breathed.

"And why, may I ask, were you reading such heavy material?" he asked.

"Mom works there now," she said matter-of-factly. "I wanted to see what kind of paper it is, whether anyone does any actual fact checking."

His mouth twitched. "And what was your analysis?"

"No evidence of yellow journalism that I could see," she replied. "But I only read a small sample of articles, so you're not free and clear yet."

Mr. Hale broke into a broad grin. It was the first time I'd seen him smile and the effect was electrifying. His whole face changed and I caught a glimpse of the man inside the vampire.

"How old are you, Marley?" he asked.

"I'm ten," she said. "I hope to come into my magic next year."

"I bet you do," he replied. "Well, in a few years, we can talk about an internship. We're always looking for sharp minds at the paper."

"So are you here to check up on me?" I asked. "You don't exactly strike me as a high school soccer fan."

He straightened the edge of his suit jacket in a well-defined move.

"I was out for a stroll and saw the game happening," he said. A likely story. "I decided to partake in the community spirit."

Marley smiled up at me. "You're right, Mom. He was checking up on you."

I placed an arm around her shoulders. "That's okay. I don't blame him. He knows perfectly well I don't know what I'm doing."

"There is a learning curve," Mr. Hale said. "I will grant you that."

"So which is it, Miss Rose?" a voice asked. "Are you training to be the new sheriff or a sports reporter?"

I turned around to see Sheriff Nash behind me. "I'm not sure what you mean," I said, although I knew exactly what he meant.

"I will thank you to stay out of my investigation," the werewolf said. A wavy chunk of dark hair dipped into his eye and I fought the urge to fix it.

"You have been talking to my suspects," he said. "Keep it up and I'll charge you with obstruction of justice. I don't care who your family is."

Mr. Hale stepped between us. "Sheriff Nash, I do believe you owe the lady an apology."

The sheriff gave him a cheeky grin. "Is that so? Tell me, Alec. How have I offended this woman? I'm simply informing her of the law and her potential violation of it. I would think you'd like to keep your employee out of jail. Am I right?"

Mr. Hale moved to stand beside me. "As it happens, Miss Rose is writing a piece on the Maiden as one of her first assignments. She has my express permission to interview any and all relevant parties."

Sheriff Nash folded his arms across his broad chest. "Do you mean to tell me a new reporter with zero experience in journalism is covering the biggest murder in Starry Hollow in years?" He clucked his tongue. "That doesn't sound like the Alec Hale that I know."

Mr. Hale stepped forward, closing the gap between them. "I said she's writing a piece on the Maiden, not on the murder. And I run the paper as I see fit. Miss Rose has shown promise. It only seems fitting to encourage her growth."

Marley jabbed me with her elbow. "I'm pretty sure he's talking about someone else," she whispered.

I shushed her and jabbed back. It was a fascinating pissing contest to watch. Although the sheriff had that unbridled werewolf machismo, Alec Hale had the coiled violence of a vampire. I felt that inner potential for swift, deadly action and it both frightened and excited me.

"Freedom of the press doesn't mean interfering with my investigation," Sheriff Nash said. "Tell your minion to stay out of it."

"She's a Rose," Mr. Hale reminded him. "She's nobody's minion."

The sheriff laughed. "That's right. How quickly I forget. We're all their minions, aren't we?"

"Speak for yourself, Sheriff Nash," Mr. Hale said. "I answer to no one."

The sheriff nodded toward me. "And yet you have a new employee that you didn't ask for. Get real, Alec. I know which side of the neck you get your blood from."

Mr. Hale scowled. "I think we're done here. Why don't you let us get back to covering the game? Readers love seeing children's names in print almost as much as they love reading a salacious murder story."

"Sure they do," the sheriff said, and turned to me. "I've got my eye on you, Miss Rose."

The sheriff marched across the open field and returned to his car in a huff.

Mr. Hale gave me a quizzical look. "He doesn't have his eye on you in that way, Miss Rose."

Color rushed to my cheeks. Damn vampire psychic. I really needed those tips on shielding my thoughts.

"I wasn't...I didn't..." I waved my hand. "Oh, forget it."

Mr. Hale smiled again and I caught a glimpse of fang. His second smile in one meeting. A record.

"So what exactly have you been up to that I don't know about?" he asked.

I gave an exasperated sigh. I was hoping to snoop around undetected. "I spoke to Garland, the Maiden's herbology partner. Until the sheriff clears my name, the Council of Elders says I can't get a passport."

"I see." Mr. Hale adjusted his tie. "Who else do you need to speak with in connection with the murder?"

My ears perked up. "Are you offering to help me?"

"It would be in my interest as editor-in-chief," he said. "Tell me and I'll help make the arrangements."

I cocked an eyebrow. "Why would you do that for me? How do you know I'm innocent?"

He tapped the side of his head. "Vampire psychic, remember?"

Right. "I'm going to see her friend Uri this evening," I said. "So maybe the High Priestess?"

He choked back a laugh. "You think the High Priestess is a suspect?"

I shrugged. "I didn't say that. But she is someone I'd like to talk to since Fleur shadowed her."

He seemed impressed. "You're a brave young woman, Miss Rose. I'll grant you that."

"Why? Is the High Priestess intimidating?" She didn't seem intimidating at my induction ceremony.

"Not at all," Mr. Hale replied. "Iris Sandstone is a lovely witch. I've known her for many years. I was just referring to your willingness to jump headfirst into a situation without fully understanding it."

"I find it best to work under the guise of ignorance," I said.

"Yeah," Marley interjected. "Ignorance really works for her. It's kind of her thing."

Mr. Hale's mouth twitched again. "It's been very nice meeting you, Marley."

"You, too, Mr. Hale," Marley said.

"Please, call me Alec."

My brows shot up. "Me, too?"

His eyes narrowed. "No, you may call me Mr. Hale."

I tried to hide my disappointment. So my ten-year-old was on a first-name basis with my vampire boss, but I was in the formal zone? Whatever.

"Let me know when you're ready and I'll reach out to Iris," Mr. Hale said.

"Okay, thanks." I watched as he crossed the field, drawing the eyes of most female spectators, and a few of the men as well. Not that I blamed them. Where Sheriff Nash was raw sexuality, Alec Hale was raw sensuality.

"So that's a vampire, huh?" Marley inquired. "He seems really fancy."

"Not so fancy that *you* can't call him by his first name."

"It's because he's trying to keep you at arm's length," Marley said.

I shot her a quizzical look. "That sounds too insightful for a ten-year-old."

Marley shrugged. "It's probably his way of maintaining distance from his employees. I'm not an employee."

Right. Distance from an employee. It was so sensible, I almost believed it myself. Almost.

CHAPTER 13

URI'S ART class took place directly on Balefire Beach, so Marley and I took PP3 for a walk, and I left them to play nearby while I spoke with Uri.

The beach itself was incredibly wide and almost white— very different from the Jersey shore. I bet the residents of Starry Hollow didn't have to contend with raw sewage washing up on the beach. They probably had a magical filter that kept the ocean looking as pristine as it did right now.

There were about a dozen easels set up in the sand in view of the horizon. I easily identified Uri—not because I recognized a vampire on sight, but because he was, by far, the saddest-looking artist in the group. Still processing his friend's death, no doubt.

I removed my shoes and let my bare feet sink into the warm sand. The sensation was heavenly.

"That's a beautiful picture," I said, moving to stand behind Uri. I didn't know anything about art, but the image was pleasing to my eye.

Uri craned his neck to look at me. His eyes were so dark, they nearly matched his black hair. He wasn't pale like

Victorine, though. Instead, his skin was more bronzed like Mr. Hale's. When I'd asked Linnea about vampires walking around in the daytime, she said it's because Starry Hollow is a paranormal town. Apparently, the paranormal towns are equipped with some kind of magical juju that allows vampires to move around in sunlight without burning to a crisp.

"Thank you," he said. "It's more melancholy than I normally like to paint, but it seems fitting under the circumstances."

"I assume you're talking about your friend, Fleur?"

He gave me a sad smile. "I'm glad you referred to her by her name and not as the Maiden." A scowl marred his smooth features. "I am so tired of hearing her reduced to a title. She was a person, not a vessel."

An interesting opinion for a vampire. "I understand you two were good friends. Her death must have hit you pretty hard." Especially as someone who didn't need to worry about a natural death.

He winced. "That's an understatement. There's a hole in my heart that will never be filled. Fleur has been my closest companion since childhood. We spent most of our free time together."

"You're such an interesting pair," I said. "I imagine your friendship must've raised a few eyebrows over the years."

He lifted his paintbrush and returned his attention to the canvas. "That's because you're from the human world, Miss Rose. You don't understand a paranormal place like Starry Hollow. Maybe you will in time, if you keep an open mind."

So he knew who I was. "I'm happy to be enlightened, Uri. So are you telling me that Starry Hollow is one big, happy paranormal family? Everyone gets along and it's all unicorns and butterflies?" I was surprised by my use of the phrase 'unicorns and butterflies.' Typically, I said something like 'puppies and rainbows.' The residents of Starry Hollow were rubbing off on me.

"I'm not trying to paint a perfect picture," he said, and took note of his canvas. "Okay, maybe I literally am trying to paint a perfect picture, but in terms of this conversation, it's not unusual for a vampire and a witch to be friends. Look around at the students in this art class."

I surveyed the small group. "They all look like humans to me. I wouldn't really know whether I was looking at were-wolves or vampires or witches."

"That's my point," he said. "You can't tell and it doesn't matter. Fleur and I became fast friends during a coloring session in first grade. There was only one black crayon and we both wanted to use it. None of the other children wanted to color with black." He smiled at the memory. "It was during our dark phase. We ended up breaking the crayon in half and sharing it."

"And you were friends ever since?"

He nodded. "We supported each other through a number of difficult times."

"Any recent ones that you'd care to share?"

He swiveled to face me. "Why are you interested in this? Is it because you're the one who found her?"

"I'm writing a piece on Fleur for *Vox Populi*," I said.

"Oh," he said, his dark eyes narrowing. "You mean the weekly paper owned by your family."

Hmm. Now he was going to throw nepotism in my face? I decided to switch gears.

"Listen, Uri. It's my first assignment and I'm trying in vain not to mess it up, so could you help me out? Since you were her best friend, do you have any theories on who may have killed her?"

His jaw tightened. "I wish I did. It would take a coven of witches to keep my fangs at bay."

"What about jealousy?" I asked. Even though Garland's jealousy didn't qualify, that didn't mean there wasn't some other seething witch in the background.

He turned back to his painting. "She was often annoyed by Ianthe, and so was I, for that matter."

"Who's Ianthe?"

"Her understudy," he replied. "Just like the Maiden is the understudy of the High Priestess, Ianthe was the understudy of the Maiden." He grew quiet. "The understudy is prepared and steps into the Maiden's role in case something like this happens."

All about Eve, coven-style. "Is Ianthe a student at the high school?"

"She attends the Black Cloak Academy," he said. "Ianthe is all about doing things the coven way. She's very different from Fleur."

"I'll speak to her then. Thanks, Uri. I appreciate your help."

I watched as he put the finishing touches on the painting. A splash of orange and red in the heart of the picture. Although the resulting image was beautiful, it made me feel sad when I looked at it. I was pretty sure that was the point.

The Mistress-of-Runecraft was a witch called Hazel and she had more freckles than I'd ever seen on a single body. Her curly red hair was cut just below the ear and her smile reminded me of a crazed clown.

Hazel arrived at the cottage with an oversized book. She swept into the room with efficient energy and set the book on the dining room table. We'd decided to hold our sessions while Marley was at school to minimize distractions. Aunt Hyacinth made sure that Mr. Hale agreed to frequent absences for the sake of my education. I was sure everyone in the office would be thrilled to learn about my special treatment. Nothing like making friends with co-workers by being labeled the special snowflake.

"What exactly is runecraft?" I asked, reading the title of the book—The Big Book of Runecraft. Very original.

"Think of it as a magical alphabet," Hazel said, opening the book to the first chapter. "It's basically learning a new language." She peered at me. "Do you speak any other languages?"

"I know Spanish curse words," I said. "Does that count?"

"No," she said, and gave me a disapproving look. She pointed to markings on the page. "I'll be teaching you how to interpret these characters and symbols."

"When would I need to know this information? Like in what context? Are the bathroom signs only marked with runes?" Because that could easily end in embarrassment.

"When it's time to have your own grimoire, you'll need to learn how to read the spells," Hazel said. "Many spells are written in runes."

"Do I need to learn spells?" I asked, staring at the black symbols on the page. I wasn't sure I'd ever be able to translate these into words. Runecraft seemed more up Marley's alley than mine.

Hazel stared at me like I'd called her baby ugly. "You don't want to learn spells?"

"I want to learn magic," I said. "Does it have to come from a spell?" Spells seemed like hard work. The type of magic that happened in the tow truck just popped out of me. Much simpler.

"No, of course not," Hazel said. "It's just that spells help us focus our magic. They set parameters."

That sounded reasonable. "Okay, so how do we do this?"

Hazel set a piece of paper in front of me. "Not much different from learning your ABC's. I'd like you to copy the symbols and characters you see on this page and write them on your paper."

I blanched. "Seriously?"

"Seriously. It's how we learn."

"It's how we learn to *draw*," I said. "But I have no clue what they mean."

"You will in time," Hazel said. "As long as you're willing to put in the work."

I shrugged. "I guess we'll find out." I picked up a pen and began to copy the first symbol. I had to admit, as silly as it felt, even this was an improvement over repossessing cars.

"Try to copy it exactly," Hazel said, tapping the paper. "You need a bit more of a curve on that one."

"What? Or I might accidentally open a gate to hell or something?"

"Might do," Hazel replied, and my eyes widened.

"Really?"

"No." She snapped her fingers and a bottle of white-out appeared on the table. "I think you'll be needing this."

"Gee, thanks for the vote of confidence." I continued working. "So do you make house calls often?"

"Rarely," Hazel admitted. "You're obviously a special case. I tend to stick to the classroom."

"Starry Hollow High School?"

"No, the Black Cloak Academy."

I frowned. "Fleur Montbatten was a witch. Why didn't she attend the academy? I would think it would be a requirement for the Maiden."

"Not all witches attend the academy," Hazel said. "Fleur insisted on mixing with other paranormals after middle school. She didn't want to be sequestered."

I could understand that. "I know she was best friends with a vampire. Is that why?"

"Maybe," Hazel said. "She and Uri were friends from

elementary school. I know she'd made it very clear to her parents that she would not attend the academy. She thought it would make her a more well-rounded witch to have a wide circle of peers."

"What about Fleur's parents?" I asked. "Weren't they suspicious of a good-looking vampire always hanging out with their beautiful daughter?"

"They were used to Uri's presence," Hazel explained. "He and Fleur were always in and out of his house or hers. If anything, I think they felt safer knowing that she had a vampire to protect her from any potential harm."

"Fleur was a badass witch," I said. "Couldn't she protect herself?"

Hazel looked amused. "I don't think anyone ever referred to Fleur as a badass. She was a sweet girl. Although she had the potential to do great magic, she would have been terrified to hurt another living being, even in self-defense."

"Then what's the point of having all that power?" I asked.

"There's more to magic than power," Hazel said. "That's a lesson you need to learn early on, if you expect to be the best witch you can be."

"I don't know what kind of witch I expect to be," I said. "I'm still coming to terms with the fact that I am one."

"Focus on the formation of the characters," Hazel said, tapping the paper again.

I studied the marks in the book. They were all so foreign to me. I may as well have been writing in Chinese.

"So there's something I don't get," I said. "Uri's a vampire, right? How has he aged from elementary school? Was he turned as a teenager?"

Hazel burst into laughter. "Sticks and wicks, you really don't know anything, do you?"

"Why would I? This whole thing is new to me."

"If you're a turned vampire, then you stop aging from

then on, and it's all the usual blood and immortality. If two vampires love each other very much, and decide to get married and produce fruit..."

"Produce fruit?" I queried. "We're not talking about groceries, Hazel. I'm a twenty-eight-year-old mother. You can say the word sex. Or fornicate. Or doing the dirty deed. Whatever gets the point across."

Hazel's expression grew pinched. "A child of two vampires will also be a vampire, but with slight differences. They do age, albeit slowly. But all the other tricks of the trade apply."

"How can a vampire produce offspring if they're undead?" I asked. I was no biology expert, but it seemed to me that if vampires couldn't breathe, they couldn't procreate.

"The relevant parts are still in working order," she said. "Generally speaking."

I chewed on the end of my pen. "So I could have a vampire baby?"

"You're not a vampire, dear," Hazel said.

"But what if I got pregnant by a vampire?" Not that I had a particular exceedingly handsome and well-dressed vampire in mind for dirty deeds.

"Then you would have one heck of an ankle biter," Hazel quipped.

I pointed my pen at her. "So you do have a sense of humor. I wasn't sure."

Hazel ignored my remark. "The offspring of a vampire and a witch can be either-or."

"Either a vampire or a witch?" Like Linnea's werewolf kids. "So I could have a vampire daughter and a wizard son?" Plus my existing soon-to-be witch daughter.

"Theoretically," Hazel said. "Why? Have you met a vampire you fancy?"

"No, no," I said quickly. "Just thinking about getting laid...

I mean, getting the lay of the land." Heat burned the back of my neck. I was suddenly grateful that Mr. Hale wasn't within mind-reading distance.

I spent the next hour filling the paper with runes. Hazel was not impressed with my chicken scratch.

"It's my first attempt," I argued. "What did you expect? A prodigy?"

"You're a descendant of the One True Witch," Hazel said. "Perhaps I did expect a bit more natural ability."

"For scribbling?" I glanced over my handiwork. It wasn't so terrible, was it?

"I'll see you next week," Hazel said, collecting her Big Book of Scribbles. "Do try to practice between now and then."

"I'll see if I can work it into my busy schedule," I replied.

Prescott Peabody III barked and jumped in front of the door.

"How sweet," Hazel said. "He's telling me goodbye."

"No, he's telling me it's time to pick up Marley from school," I said, and I grabbed his leash. "Let's go, buddy. We'll walk Hazel to the gate."

After dropping Marley and PP3 at the cottage, I headed to the academy to follow up on Hazel's intel. I spotted the pretty blonde talking to a group of boys. Each one seemed more enamored than the next. Why did the next Maiden need to be a pretty blonde, too? It only served to reinforce a beauty stereotype. I smoothed my own dark hair before approaching the group.

"Hi, are you Ianthe?"

The group turned to look at me.

"Yes," she said. "That's me." Her voice was surprisingly childlike. It reminded me of Marilyn Monroe.

"My name's Ember and I work for the local newspaper. Do you mind if I ask you a few questions?"

Her smile brightened. She probably thought I was here to do a cover story on her. Well, let her think that. She'd be more forthcoming that way.

"Of course," she said. "I'd be happy to answer any questions you have." She faced her group of admirers. "We'll talk later guys, okay?"

I wondered whether her bevy of admirers realized they had no chance of getting into her pants. Certainly not now that she was the new Maiden.

"What's the story about?" Ianthe asked, once we were out of earshot of the others.

"I understand you're going to be sworn in as the new Maiden soon," I said. I bit the inside of my cheek. Sworn in? She wasn't going to be appointed as a judge. I had no clue what the right terminology was.

"Yes, that's correct," she said. She was as poised as a beauty pageant contestant. "There will be an official coven ceremony to appoint me."

"I understand you were Fleur Montbatten's understudy," I said. "What was that like?"

"Fleur and I were great friends," she said. "I've been devastated ever since her death."

Sure. She looked positively depressed while talking to those boys.

"How disappointed were you to be the bridesmaid and not the bride?"

Ianthe cocked her head. "I don't understand. Who was going to be a bride?"

I tried again. "The fact that you would never be the Maiden, just the understudy. Did that bother you? You were essentially the runner-up in a beauty pageant. The name no one remembers."

Her expression grew serious. "The role of Maiden is nothing like being a beauty pageant contestant," she said. "She serves the High Priestess. It's a very important position and nothing to speak lightly of. For a reporter, it doesn't sound like you've done very much research."

Consider me shamed. "Please feel free to educate me. I'm new to this whole scene, so forgive me if I'm not as knowledgeable as I should be."

The *mea culpa* seemed to win her over.

"If the Mother is the soul of the coven, and the Crone is the mind, then think of the Maiden as the heart. Nothing survives without a heart."

"I see. While we're on the subject of hearts, do you have a boyfriend?"

Ianthe balked. "Certainly not. The minute I knew I'd be the Maiden's understudy, I pledged a vow to remain chaste. It's much easier to keep the vow when you don't tempt fate."

"You certainly had a lot of male admirers when I got here," I said. "Do they know you're off the market?"

"Yes, of course," she said firmly. "I *want* to be the Maiden."

Exactly, but how badly? Enough to kill?

"You don't mind forgoing…the, um, pleasures of the flesh?" Pleasures of the flesh? Did I seriously just say that? Kill me now.

"It isn't forever," Ianthe said. "Once I age out of the role, I'll either take over as High Priestess or be free to turn in my circlet."

"Age out?" Suddenly she sounded like a Hollywood actress.

Ianthe nodded. "The celibacy doesn't last forever." Her expression grew somber. "Though I may miss out on my childbearing years, depending on the timeline."

Ouch. "So you might be the Maiden into your forties?"

"So much depends on the High Priestess," Ianthe said.

"Whether she wants to retire, step down, take on a new role...It won't be up to me."

It sounded far too political for my taste.

"When's the last time you saw Fleur?" I asked.

"The day before she died," Ianthe replied. "We had lunch in town. We made plans to work on spells together in the evening, but she never showed."

"Where were you supposed to meet?"

"The academy library. It's open in the evenings for students, but very few take advantage of the late hours."

"Did you tell anyone that she didn't show?"

"No. I texted her, but she didn't respond." She shrugged. "It wasn't unusual for her to bail on me. I assumed she decided to hang out with Uri instead. They spent a lot of time together."

"Were you practicing spells for a reason?"

"She had a quiz. She relied on me for help."

Like she relied on Garland for help in herbology. Interesting.

"But you're not even in the same school," I said.

"It doesn't matter," Ianthe replied. "As her understudy, it was my job to support her and I did it gladly. The spells are the same and I do more advanced spellcasting at the academy."

"If she needed your help for the quiz, why would she spend the time with Uri instead? Didn't she worry about her grades?"

Ianthe gave me a soft smile. "She didn't. Fleur always found a way to shine. She could fall in a mud puddle and emerge smelling like a rose garden. She was blessed."

"Some people are just like that," I said. I'd known a few in my lifetime. It was easy to resent that sort of luck. Although it would be easy to assume Ianthe resented it, too, I wasn't seeing any sign of it.

"If you need any pictures of Fleur for the article, I have plenty," Ianthe said. "We spent so much time together, I could paper my walls with them." Her gaze drifted to the ground. "She will be missed."

"I'm sorry for your loss," I said, and realized that I meant it. "I'll let you know about the pictures."

CHAPTER 14

"Now Mom, you're going to have to be on your best behavior," Marley warned me, as we stood in front of Aster's picture-perfect house. It was Aster's turn to host us for dinner and Marley was excited to meet her younger cousins.

I gave her a quick look. "Aren't I supposed to be saying that to you?"

Marley shrugged. "Probably. But we both know who the troublemaker is in this duo."

She wasn't wrong. I rang the doorbell and waited.

The front door open and Aster greeted us with a pearly white smile. "Come on in. We're so pleased you could make it."

It was like walking straight into the pages of a Pottery Barn catalog. The woman even had white sofas. White sofas with two little boys? What was she thinking?

Traditional was the best word to describe the interior. A place for everything and everything in its place. Linnea wasn't kidding about Aster doing everything right. Her home certainly reflected that sentiment.

"Sterling and the boys are just upstairs. They'll be down any minute."

I noticed that she didn't yell up to them the way Linnea or I might have done. She simply waited patiently.

"May I offer you anything to drink? I have juniper juleps for the grown-ups." She beamed at Marley. "And mickleberry fizzes for the children."

"What's a mickleberry fizz?" Marley asked, scrunching her nose.

Aster's eyes grew round. "You've never had a mickleberry fizz? Marley Rose, you are in for a real treat. Follow me into the kitchen and I'll whip one up for you."

"I wouldn't object to a juniper julep," I said. Although I'd never had one, it sounded delightful.

Once they left the room, I felt free to explore. There were photographs everywhere. Frames on the walls. Frames on the sideboard. Bright, happy faces smiled back at me from within each and every frame. One photograph was of the twins' footprints from the day they were born. Tiny.

I glanced up at the sound of approaching footsteps.

"You must be the famous missing cousin," Sterling said. He gave me a welcoming smile and took my hand. "I'm Sterling Rose-Stanton, Aster's husband. I'm sorry I missed your induction ceremony. I had to work late."

Sterling looked like he could be related to Aster. An attractive man with similar coloring, he had a decent build, but the kind that came from a gym rather than physical labor. He was flanked by two little boys with the signature white-blond hair of the Roses. "This one here on the left is Ackley, and this one here on the right is Aspen."

I crouched down to greet them. "Hi, boys. I'm your cousin, Ember. My daughter, Marley, has just gone into the kitchen with your mom to get a mickleberry fizz."

The little boys were dressed adorably in small linen suits

with bowties. Instead of trousers, they wore shorts and argyle knee socks. It was, quite frankly, the cutest thing I'd ever seen on a kid.

"It's very nice to meet you, Ember," Ackley said.

"Likewise," Aspen added.

And I thought Marley was polite and well behaved. Aster was a marvel of a mother.

Ackley gazed up at his father with his bright blue eyes. "Daddy, would it be all right if I had a mickleberry fizz?"

Sterling ruffled his hair. "Go ask your mom. I'm sure if Marley is having one, then the invitation extends to you."

Both boys walked off toward the kitchen. That's right—walked. No running. And they didn't even drag their feet in that annoying way some kids did. What sorcery was this?

I stared at Sterling in amazement. "Are you drugging those children?"

Sterling gave me a beguiling look. "Aster has them trained. She's got me trained, too, as a matter of fact. The woman is a wonder."

I was inclined to agree. "Your home is gorgeous. Thornhold is nice and all, but this place manages to be both beautiful and comfortable at the same time. I don't feel like I have to sit up straight in here."

Sterling laughed. "I know what you mean. It's all down to my amazing wife. I just show up."

Aster emerged from the kitchen with a tray of drinks and set them on the coffee table.

"No magic?" I queried. Why carry a tray when magic could do it for you?

"We try to keep things as normal as possible here," Aster explained.

"Why?" I asked. "You live in Starry Hollow. It's not like you're trying to blend in with humans."

"We discussed this before the children were born. We

don't know what the boys will choose in life at this point," Aster said. "If they don't want to stay in a place like Starry Hollow, I need them to learn how the human world works. How to live without magic. Since they won't come into their magic for another seven years, it seems like the perfect time to train them."

Talk about forward thinking. I had to hand it to Aster. Those kids will be prepared for life.

"So I have an awkward question," I began.

Marley groaned. "Mom, if you already know it's awkward, then why are you asking?"

"Not to worry, Marley," Aster said. "We're family. Your mother should feel free to ask any question she likes."

Marley's eyes widened to the size of walnuts. "You are treading on dangerous ground with that statement."

I plowed ahead. "I keep hearing people refer to you as Aster Rose-Muldoon, but Sterling and the boys are Rose-Stanton. What's up with that?"

Sterling plucked a drink from the tray and took a sip. "It's typical in this coven for the witch's name to carry on down the bloodline, especially descendants of the One True Witch. I was Sterling Stanton-Craig growing up, but once I married Aster, I dropped my father's name and combined my mother's with Rose."

"That's so cool," Marley said. "It's kind of like what you did, Mom. You kept your maiden name."

"That's just because I was too lazy to change anything," I said.

Marley swallowed her mickleberry fizz in two minutes flat. I'd never seen her drink anything so quickly outside of chocolate milk.

"How do you like your juniper julep?" Aster asked.

"It's surprisingly refreshing," I said.

"They really are," she replied, appearing pleased. "Many

families in Starry Hollow prefer magical drinks, but for me, a traditional juniper julep is magical all on its own."

My curiosity was piqued. "What do you mean by magical drinks?"

"Like the ones you had at Linnea's," Marley said. "Moonglow."

"Oh. Those were magical drinks? I just thought they were normal drinks with funny names like Sex on the Beach or Rusty Nail."

Marley shook her head. "Oh, Mom."

"Seriously, though," I continued. "What makes them magical? I didn't feel anything weird after I drank it."

"It depends on the drink," Sterling explained. "In general, magical cocktails are made from fruits and other ingredients that aren't available in the human world. Burstberries, mickleberries, and fizzlewicks. Things like that."

"So mickleberry fizz is magical?" Marley asked, staring into her empty glass.

"There won't be a magical effect," Aster said, "but yes."

"Mom, may we please have a snack?" Aspen asked. Or maybe it was Ackley. It would take me more than one visit to tell them apart.

"Aspen, you are my bottomless pit," Aster said.

Okay, so Aspen wore the blue bowtie and Ackley wore the red one. Noted.

"As it happens, I have hors d'oeuvres ready in the kitchen," Aster said.

Of course she did. Magical Martha Stewart wouldn't make a hosting faux pas like no hors d'oeuvres. Me, on the other hand, would serve hors d'oeuvres as the main course. Who doesn't love mini hotdogs?

"Can I help you bring out the platters, Mom?" Ackley asked.

"Of course you can, my sweet," Aster said. She held out

her hand and he took it. "Come then, let's bring the food out for everyone to enjoy."

I had to admit, I was starting to feel a bit nauseous in the middle of all this sweetness and light. Aunt Hyacinth was put-together like Aster, but less filtered. That probably came with age, though, unless you were from New Jersey. In Aster's house, there was too much perfection. I hated to say it, but it was starting to grate on my nerves. I was desperate for one of the boys to make a fart joke.

Aster and her progeny reappeared with a platter of food.

"Oh, I love these," Marley said, picking up what appeared to be a mini burger.

I gave her a sharp look. "Where have you ever had these before?" Certainly not in my apartment. The only culinary skills happening in there were on the television screen during a cooking show.

I took a bite of one and the taste exploded in my mouth. It was insanely good.

"Popcorn balls," I said.

"No, silly," Aster said. "These aren't popcorn balls. They're crab cake sliders."

I waved her off. "No, it's just an expression." I hoped there were more of these because I could eat the whole platter by myself.

"Because swearing is so rampant in New Jersey, my mom tries very hard not to use bad language around me," Marley explained. "She's trained herself to use all of these innocent expressions."

Aster's expression shifted to one of admiration. "That's lovely, Ember. I think it's a wonderful gift to give our children, to shield them as long as we can from life's vulgarities."

I raised a finger. "Speaking of shielding, this might be the right time to ask for some help."

Sterling's brow lifted. "What kind of help?"

"You know I'm working at the paper," I said. "My boss, Mr. Hale…"

Aster shuddered. "Yes, we know Alec Hale."

"He seems to be able to read my thoughts, or at least snippets of them. He said I should learn to shield them. How do I do that?"

"Yes, we can definitely help you with that," Aster said. "Sterling and I are master shielders, aren't we?"

Sterling nodded in agreement. "That we are, my darling."

"I don't blame you for wanting to protect your thoughts from him," Aster said. "I'm sure you're deathly frightened of him. He's a very intimidating man. Vampires generally are, but Alec seems to make a sport of it."

Intimidating wasn't quite the word I was thinking of, but I decided to keep that nugget to myself.

"How about after dinner?" Aster asked. "Once the children are occupied with dessert."

Marley lit up. "Did someone say dessert?"

I wrapped my arm around her shoulders and gave her a squeeze. "My little sweet tooth. You come by it honestly."

We polished off the hors d'oeuvres and moved into the dining room for dinner. There was not a speck of dust or a knickknack out of place in that room either. I didn't know how she managed to keep the house so orderly with two four-year-old boys and a working husband without the use of magic. It wasn't like Aster sat at home all day doing nothing. From what I gathered, she served on the board of many committees. She was taking her role as a Rose-Muldoon very seriously, unlike her siblings.

The dining room was just as warm and inviting as the rest of the house. The long rectangular table was made of white oak and impeccably set. The cutlery was wrapped in a crisp white linen cloth and fastened with silver moon napkin rings.

"You're welcome to come and set the table at my house anytime," I said. Marley was lucky if I remembered to rip off a couple of paper towels to stand in as napkins.

Aster took her place at one end of the table, her sense of pride evident.

Sterling returned from the kitchen, holding two large platters of food. He set one down in front of his wife and brought the other one to his end of the table.

"I hope you like sea bass," Aster said. "I tried to choose a safe option since it's your first time dining here."

Marley was practically salivating. "I can't wait to try everything."

She couldn't wait to try sea bass? I hardly recognized this child. As perfect as she was, she was not an adventurous eater. Starry Hollow seemed to have triggered something in her.

Dinner consisted of polite and mildly amusing conversation. Aster finished two juniper juleps and started on a third. Her mother's daughter. It was how I imagined dinner parties went in the human world, when people were getting to know each other. I'd never been to an actual dinner party, so my only frame of reference was from television and movies.

Once everyone's plates were cleared, Aster sent the children off to play. "A little break before dessert is always a good idea," she said.

I remained at the table with Aster and Sterling.

"Can I interest you in any tea or coffee?" Aster queried.

"I'm good with water," I said.

"Marley seems like a wonderful girl," Sterling said. "You must be very proud."

"I am, but I can't take any credit for her," I said. "She was born like Athena out of that guy's head. Fully formed and amazing."

Sterling grinned. "You mean Zeus?"

"Yeah, that guy," I said. "I can never remember his name. Marley told me about him one time. She likes mythology."

"Well, that will certainly come in handy in Starry Hollow," Aster said. "Was there no part of you that was ever drawn to mythology and folklore? I would've thought the magic would have been calling to you all these years."

"I'll be honest, I have given it a bit of thought," I said. "I think it's because I was so focused on survival. Who has time to dwell on gods and goddesses when you're worried about feeding your child and paying your rent? Even before my husband died, we weren't exactly rolling in dough. We were always worried about money. I was pregnant when I gradu-ated high school, so I wasn't able to get a job right away."

Aster and Sterling fell silent for a moment, probably counting their many blessings.

"I'm sorry. Did I overshare?" I had a tendency to do that.

"Not at all," Aster said. "I told you before. We're family. You should always feel free to say anything you like."

Somehow, Aster didn't strike me as the unrestrained type. She was far too polished.

"So you want to learn about shielding your thoughts," Sterling said. "It's quite simple, really. You just need to exer-cise it like a muscle."

"Eventually it will be automatic," Aster added. "Your mind will do it with no conscious effort."

"No conscious effort?" I queried. "That's right up my alley."

Aster wore a vague smile. "You seem harder on yourself than you deserve."

Although I disagreed, I didn't want to argue with my cousin at her lovely dinner party. I might not be invited back and the food was too delicious to risk it.

"So pretend I'm Mr. Hale," Sterling said.

While Sterling was reasonably attractive, it was hard to

picture him as the chiseled and sensual vampire. Sterling's good looks were more all-American, whereas Alec Hale's were of the devastatingly handsome variety.

"Now visually wrap your mind in a cloak," Sterling said. "Choose a black cloak. It makes it easier to imagine."

I closed my eyes and tried to picture it.

"Whatever thoughts you're holding at the moment, keep them protected inside the cloak," Sterling continued. "Treat them like precious cargo that can't be trusted with anyone else."

"When I was learning," Aster began, "I liked to pretend I was a spy in enemy territory and I'd been captured. I would practice keeping my state secrets in my mental cloak. Knowing it was a life or death situation made it somewhat easier."

Sterling broke into a grin. "You never told me that."

Aster shrugged and gesticulated, nearly knocking over her empty julep glass. "There's a lot about me I haven't told you. We have many years left together. Probably best to leave some surprises, don't you think?"

"I quite like the idea of playing spy," Sterling said with a mischievous glint in his eye.

Oh, man. I did not need to be here for sexy times between a married couple. Maybe we'd have to skip dessert. Marley would be disappointed, but the alternative was much worse.

"So pretend I'm Alec Hale and I'm standing next to your desk, demanding you finish typing up your piece by the deadline," Sterling said. "You have negative thoughts about this, but you don't want Alec to hear them."

I wrapped my negative thoughts in the black cloak. It was hard to know whether I was successful without having a mind reader in the room. Still, it was helpful to have a method that I could practice at home.

We went a few more rounds before Aster decided it was

time to serve dessert. She rang a silver bell like the one her mother used. Again, I heard no sound. Moments later, the boys appeared in the dining room and I cackled like the witch I apparently was.

"Gods above," Sterling sputtered, staring at them.

Although the boys still wore their linen shorts and knee socks, their top halves were covered in what I assumed was Aster's lacy lingerie. Their faces were fully made up, including bright red lipstick. Marley appeared behind them, looking chagrin.

"I'm sorry," she said. "I tried to stop them, but they were maniacs. There were more arms and legs than I could handle and then the cat jumped into the drawer..."

Aster balked. "Viola was in the drawer?"

"You should see her familiar, Mom," Marley said. "She's so pretty. You've never seen yellow like this on a cat." Marley hesitated. "I'm sorry, Aster, but she may have gotten yellow cat hair on some of your black underwear."

"Ackley and Aspen Rose-Stanton," Aster said, her tone low and threatening.

"It was Aspen's idea," Ackley said, pointing.

"You know you're not allowed in my drawers," Aster said.

"It's a good thing we found these," Aspen said. "I think you need to throw them away."

"Why is that?" Aster asked, her eyes narrowing.

"Look at the holes everywhere," Aspen said, poking his finger through the lace. "I think the moths got to them."

Aster's pale skin glowed red. "Take those items off carefully and place them on my bed, please. Now."

"We may have also knocked over your lamp," Ackley said.

Aster's eyes bulged. "Which lamp?"

"The pineapple one," Aspen said.

I didn't want to ask Marley what she was doing during all

of this. I knew her too well to think she was involved in the shenanigans.

"Calm down, Aster," Sterling said. "It's nothing a little magic can't fix."

I was pretty sure I saw steam flowing from Asters' ears. "Sterling, you know perfectly well that goes against everything we're trying to teach the boys."

"Magic, magic," the boys began to chant in unison.

Sterling gave her a lopsided grin. "From the mouths of babes."

"You know what?" I said. "It's getting late. Marley and I should go. Our dog will need to go out for a walk before bedtime."

"But Mom..." Marley began and I knew she was going to ask about dessert.

"Not now, Marley," I said.

Aster pushed back her chair. She looked close to tears. "I'm sorry, Marley. Let me send dessert home with you. I can wrap it up quickly with magic."

"Magic, magic," the boys chanted again.

Aster's head whipped around like the little girl in *The Exorcist*. "Not another word out of you two or you'll be drinking bile from a lizard's eye socket tonight."

The twins paled and clamped their mouths closed. For all of her beauty and polish, Aster had a tough streak that resembled her mother's. Now that I'd seen it, I'd never forget it.

Aster relaxed her shoulders. She turned back to us and flashed her pearly whites. "Now let me get that dessert to go, shall I?"

CHAPTER 15

THE STARRY HOLLOW Broomstick Tour ran twice a day, once at noon and once at four. Each tour lasted forty minutes.

"I'm not sure about this," Marley said, gripping my hand.

"It'll be fine," I replied. "It's like a ride at an amusement park."

"I hate rides. You know that."

"We'll ride the same broom. Come on, it'll be fun. We'll get to see the town from a completely different perspective, like one of those helicopter tours over New York City."

"Didn't one of those crash?"

I hugged her tightly. "Marley Rose, you will survive the Starry Hollow Broomstick Tour, even if it kills me."

"Yes, that's exactly what I'm worried about."

I sighed loudly and stepped up to the counter to purchase our tickets.

"Skilled or unskilled?" the man behind the counter asked.

"Um, skilled in some ways," I said. Like repossessing cars, and I could leap a fence like nobody's business.

He pointed upward. "Do you have experience riding a broom?"

"Oh, no. Two unskilled tickets."

He tore off two orange tickets and I gave him the money.

"You'll need to join the line on the left," he said.

Each line had about six people already waiting. We joined the unskilled line, and I had to assume we were the only witches in it since most witches were probably adept broom riders.

"Are we ready for the four o'clock tour?" a woman asked. She looked familiar--I was fairly certain she'd attended my induction ceremony.

The crowd responded eagerly.

"Excellent. Skilled riders will choose their brooms first," she said. "Then I'll have the unskilled riders come over."

We waited patiently for our turn. The woman smiled broadly when she saw me approach.

"How lovely to see you here," she said. "I'm not sure if you remember me from your ceremony. My name is Lotus."

I vaguely remembered meeting a Lotus. "Yes, hi. This is my daughter, Marley."

"Welcome to Starry Hollow," she said. "Although most people here are tourists, this tour is a great way to get to know your new home."

"That's why we're here," I said. "Can we ride together?"

"Absolutely," she said. "I'll make sure you have the beginner broom. Don't want you streaking across the sky into human airspace."

"No, we don't want that either," I replied. Marley gripped my hand and squeezed. Hard. "Lotus, my daughter has some concerns. It's perfectly safe, isn't it?"

Lotus gave Marley a reassuring smile. "Of course it is. Just don't let go and, if you feel nauseous, don't look down. And don't wave to anyone." She started to move away, but suddenly turned back again. "And don't try to look behind you or you might lose your balance."

"Um, thank you, Lotus," I said, and steered Marley to the rows of hanging broomsticks.

"How about this pink one?" I asked, trying to distract her from the list of potential dangers.

"Mom, you know I don't like pink."

"Right. Sorry. There was a time when you did, you know? You may not remember, but I do."

"Here." She snatched a turquoise broomstick from the hook. "This one looks good."

We huddled with the rest of the tourists on the dock marked 'Tours.'

"Are we going out over the water?" Marley whispered, and I heard the anxiety in her voice.

Lotus clapped her hands. "If I can have everyone's attention, please. I'm going to run through the basic rules and help any of our unskilled riders who require assistance. Then we'll be on our way. Sound good?"

People murmured their assent. Lotus ran through the instructions and rules with more precision than any flight attendant I'd ever seen on TV. I felt a rise of excitement when I realized that we were about to ride a broomstick over Starry Hollow. A broomstick!

Marley was told to sit in front of me and I would steer the broomstick from behind her by holding a leather strap.

"Now these broomsticks are all imbued with magic so you don't need to be a magic user in order to ride one," Lotus said. "My broomstick is bright red with the Silver Moon flag flying at the back. I'll be at the front of the pack so keep an eye on me."

We sailed into the air, higher and higher, until the figures below were mere specks. The breeze ripped through my hair and I knew I'd look like a rabid cavewoman by the time we landed. As we flew over the town, I periodically poked Marley in the side to make sure she was okay.

"Stop poking me, Mom," she insisted. "I'm fine."

"Are your eyes open?"

She hesitated. "Maybe."

I poked her again. "Open your eyes, you're missing all the good stuff."

The view of the ocean would have been enough, but as it happened, Starry Hollow was just as charming from above as it was from the ground. I didn't know much about architecture, but I recognized pretty buildings when I saw them. And the buildings in Starry Hollow were among the prettiest I'd ever seen.

As the sun warmed my skin, I realized how much I enjoyed being airborne. When I was younger, I remembered a conversation I had with a friend about our desired superpowers. Hers was invisibility and mine was the ability to fly. Maybe I knew something deep down.

"Mom, look at that fountain," Marley said.

Good. That meant her eyes were open. I followed the turn of her head to see a huge fountain on the ground below. Even from this distance, I could see seven statues with water gushing from a variety of places.

"Mom, the statues are moving!"

They were. The fountain statues were changing position before our eyes. Magic at work.

"Can we go and see that when we're on the ground?" Marley asked.

"I don't know about today," I said. "Remember, Marley. There's plenty of time to scope things out. We live here now."

"I know," she said. "Isn't it crazy?"

It really was. Starry Hollow was beyond my wildest imagination. It was a cross between an artsy beach town and Diagon Alley. I knew that we'd barely scratched the magical surface at this point. There would be ample time to get to know more of the town. I had no doubt that Aunt Hyacinth would make sure of that.

"Look at that statue on top of that building," Marley said, as we swooped close enough for a decent view. The statue was of a witch. She wore a cloak and her feet were bare. A crown was carved into her head like the one I'd seen the High Priestess wear during my induction ceremony. In her hands, she held a disk up to the sky. A silver moon, presumably.

"Do you think that building is the coven headquarters?" Marley asked.

"That's a good possibility," I said.

As we soared over more of the town, I was amazed by the ease with which I flew the broom. It was as simple and natural as riding a bicycle. I wondered whether it was the same for all witches.

"There's Fairy Cove," Marley said, and I saw the curve of the shoreline not far from the lighthouse. "Kids from school like to swim there."

From this vantage point, I could see the newspaper office with its unobstructed view of the water. I wondered whether Mr. Hale was in there right now, polishing his cufflinks. Silly me, I was sure he had a minion do that for him.

The group of broomsticks turned, so we turned with them.

"I think we're heading back to the dock now," Marley said.

"Looks that way."

For a moment, I was concerned about my landing skills, but everything turned out fine. The broomstick basically landed itself. Marley and I climbed off without a hitch. No sooner did my feet touch the ground than Marley's arms were wrapped around my waist. I squeezed her tightly.

"Are you okay?" I asked.

She jumped up and down in my arms. "That was amazing. Can we do it again?"

My heart soared. My anxious child wanted to fly on a broomstick again. "Another time."

Lotus came over to check on us. "As soon as your mother gets her broomstick license, she can take you up whenever you like."

"A broomstick license?" I queried. "Like a driver's license?"

Lotus nodded. "That's right. It's standard for witches and wizards. Once you get your passport, you'll be able to take a test and get your license."

I groaned inwardly. Another layer of bureaucracy to overcome.

"Mom, can I help you pick out a broomstick when it's time?"

I hugged her again. "Of course you can. I know you wouldn't steer me wrong. Get it? Steer me?"

Marley moaned and rolled her eyes. "No mom jokes. My stomach is already nauseous from the flight."

Lotus pulled a vial from her pocket and popped off the lid. She held it beneath Marley's nostrils. "Breathe this in and you'll feel better."

Marley inhaled deeply and smiled. "Wow. My nausea is gone. What is that?"

Lotus popped the lid back on. "A magical elixir I keep on hand for tours. You're not the only one who gets nauseous. Sometimes, we get worse than that, so consider yourself lucky."

I considered *myself* lucky in that case. After all, I was the one riding the broomstick with her.

"Do you think you can manage a bite to eat?" I asked. "I saw a restaurant from the sky that looked pretty cool. It's at the top of the lighthouse. I think the room revolves."

"It does," Lotus confirmed. "It's a very popular place to eat. The lobster mac-n-cheese is divine."

Marley's eyes lit up. "Can I try that?"

I couldn't believe my ears. "You want to eat lobster?"

"If it's in mac-n-cheese, then yes."

I wasn't about to argue. For the first time in her life since she ate strained carrots out of a jar, Marley seemed eager to try new things. I didn't care how much it cost to eat there, I was willing to splurge.

I rang the bell of the separate entrance for Florian's man cave. The door creaked open, but no one was there to greet me.

"Hello?" I called.

"Come on down, Ember," Florian's voice drifted back to me.

I took the modern metal staircase down to an open loft area. The first thing I spotted was a pool table in the middle of the room. Florian leaned against it, a pool cue in his hand.

"Solo game?" I asked.

"I find it relaxing," he said.

Because his life was *so* stressful. It was rough being the rich man-baby of a famous family of witches and wizards.

"This place is better than a Tribeca loft," I said. Or so I imagined.

The interior walls were brick and there was a basketball hoop attached to the far wall. Two sofas made of light gray leather sat in the middle of the room and there was a surfboard propped up against the wall behind them.

"That floating staircase is cool," I said, gesturing behind me.

"It's not even magic," he said. "Just good architecture."

Even his kitchen managed to be masculine yet impressive.

The industrial look worked well in the space. I spotted a wine chiller built in to the lower cabinet area. A bachelor necessity.

"I can see what attracts the ladies here," I said. "This is the ultimate bachelor pad." I never would have pictured a place like this in a house like Thornhold.

"I like to think it's more than my furnishings that attract them to me," he said, raking a hand through his white-blond hair.

"Linnea said that you're into fairies at the moment," I said. "Is it a revolving door of paranormals?"

He chuckled. "For now. There's no one special at the moment."

"At the moment or forever?" I queried.

He picked up a basketball and began to dribble it on the hardwood floor. "What's the point? If I find someone special, it will only end in death or divorce."

"That's the spirit," I said, giving him a playful punch on the arm.

"You're mocking me, aren't you?"

"What makes you so negative about it?" His attitude seemed horribly jaded for someone in Florian's polished loafers.

"Look at Linnea. Look at my mother." He gestured to me. "Look at you. Even your parents. Those who marry for love seem to suffer the most."

"I noticed that you didn't mention Aster," I said. "Do you think she isn't in love with Sterling?"

He shrugged and shot the ball into the hoop. "I think they have a familial love. There's no passion there from what I can see."

"But they get along well, at least from the limited time I've spent with them," I said. "Isn't that the kind of relationship that you'd be happy with?"

"Not really." He retrieved the ball and handed it to me. "Your shot."

"I'm terrible at handling balls," I said.

He burst into laughter. "I wouldn't advertise that fact if you're in the market for a new boyfriend."

I pushed the ball into his arm. "You know what I mean. I don't think you should be afraid to put yourself out there because of what might happen. Even if I knew in advance that Karl would die an early death and leave me alone with Marley, I'd do it all the same."

He stared at me. "Would you, really?"

I took the shot and was amazed when it landed in the net. "Sometimes you get lucky. Sometimes you don't. That's just life. It doesn't mean you don't take the shot."

He grinned. "Look at you, making sports metaphors. Starry Hollow will change you yet."

I was pretty sure it already had.

"So to what do I owe the pleasure of your visit?" Florian asked. "No runecraft today?"

"Nope," I said. "I'm working on an article about Fleur for the paper."

Florian appeared surprised. "I thought Alec had you covering local sports?"

"Oh, I'm doing that, too," I said. "I ended up with this assignment because of the sheriff."

"The sheriff?" Florian shook his head. "Forget it. You don't need to explain. Alec Hale and Granger Nash in one breath says it all."

"Do you know why they dislike each other so much?"

"I've heard rumors, but you'd have to ask Linnea. She may have gotten the real story from Wyatt a while back." He dribbled the ball on the hardwood floor. "So how's the article coming along?"

"I'm stuck," I said. "I've spoken to Fleur's herbology partner, her Maiden understudy, her best friend, Uri…"

Florian choked back a laugh. "Best friend? Is that still the official story? I guess I can understand why."

I balked. "What's that supposed to mean?"

"There's no way those two were strictly platonic," Florian said. "I used to see them around town together. Trust me, I'm a guy. I know these things."

"But everyone I spoke to, even Uri…"

"Uri is just trying to be a gentleman at this point," he said. "His girlfriend is dead. Why soil her reputation now?"

"But she was the Maiden," I argued. "What would be the point of having a boyfriend if they knew they had no future as a couple?"

Florian shrugged. "Who knows? They were young and into each other. If they were anything like me, they probably weren't thinking about a future at all."

Hmm. Or maybe only one of them was. Part of me had hoped to keep a low profile and figure things out without the need to speak with anyone official, but I couldn't drag my heels any longer. It was time to seek out the High Priestess.

CHAPTER 16

I FOUND Iris Sandstone exactly where Mr. Hale said I would. It was a tough climb to the water's edge, but the payoff was worth it. The view across the water was stunning. White seagulls dotted the blue horizon—at least I assumed they were seagulls. Who knew in Starry Hollow?

Iris stood front and center, her eyes closed and her arms outstretched. She was doing some kind of yoga, although I couldn't tell you which position. My knowledge of yoga was limited to stretching and breathing.

She looked more serene than the woman I'd met during my induction ceremony. No surprise since she was alone and doing her own thing. She wore a baggy gray dress and bare feet. Her long, silver hair was partially pulled back, with the remaining hair hanging loose down her back. Around her neck she wore a simple pendant—a silver moon glistened against her chest.

I wasn't sure whether to start talking or make a noise first. I didn't want to startle her and send her flying off the edge of the cliff. The coven didn't need to lose two members after my arrival. Talk about bad timing.

"It's a beautiful view, isn't it?" Iris asked.

I squinted. Yep, her eyes were still closed. And here I thought I had magical ninja skills. Bummer.

"Did you hear me coming?" I asked.

"No, I felt you." She opened her eyes and focused on me. "Would you like to join me in a sun salutation, Ember?"

I was pretty sure that did not involve simply giving the sun a friendly wave. "I'm good, thanks."

"Many coven members find peace and serenity in yoga," she said. "Perhaps you will be one of them."

"I seriously doubt yoga is my thing," I replied. "I'm from the Northeast. We're a pretty high-strung bunch."

She gave me a relaxed smile. "Nothing that can't be unlearned." She continued her yoga, moving into another position.

"What's that one called?"

"Warrior pose," Iris said. "It's a strong pose, meant to work every muscle in your body."

Every muscle? That sounded like overkill to me. "You don't do yoga with other witches?"

"I come here most mornings alone," she said. "But I also do group sessions at The Arched Cat—it's a yoga studio on Thistle Street. I find it relaxing to start the day with only Mother Nature smiling down on me."

I generally started the day with a smelly dog staring down at me. He liked his breakfast bright and early.

"I'm not sure if you know, but I'm working for the newspaper," I said.

She shifted to a different position. "Yes, I'm aware. It didn't exactly come as a surprise. Hyacinth likes to take care of her own."

"I'll be honest. I'm grateful for it," I said. "I'm not qualified for much of anything, so the fact that she's giving me a chance to do more than make coffee is appreciated."

And I wasn't even sure I'd be that adept at making coffee.

Iris smiled at me again. "Gratitude is a good quality in anyone, particularly a witch. Giving thanks to the universe enables us to receive its many blessings."

I hesitated. "Have you always been like this?"

She tilted her head. "Like what?"

"Like this." I zigzagged my finger. "This new wave, hippie dippy, Berkeley-inspired granola act."

She laughed softly. "Some people might find your question insulting, but I'll choose not to take offense. To answer your question, yes. I've always been like this. I come from a long line of hippie dippies, as you call them."

"I wasn't trying to offend you," I said. Although in hindsight, I could see how it might be construed that way.

Iris relaxed her pose. "I know, Ember. I feel what's in your heart, and it isn't malignant."

I'm glad she could feel that, because there were days when I wasn't too sure myself.

"And what about Fleur's heart?" I asked. "Could you feel what was in hers?" If Fleur was shadowing Iris, they would have spent a lot of quality time together. Plenty of opportunity for someone as insightful as the High Priestess to sense any budding romance between Fleur and Uri.

"Fleur had a kind heart," she replied. "And she was an excellent Maiden. Her death is a great loss to the coven. Performing her funeral rites was the hardest thing I've ever done."

I was confident that Iris had deliberately misinterpreted my question. With that slight misstep, she'd given herself away. I'd have to push harder.

"How long have you known about Fleur and Uri?" Okay, so maybe my question was a little too on-the-nose.

"They've been friends since childhood," she replied

smoothly. "What's there to know?"

I moved closer and looked her in the eye. "You know what I mean, High Priestess."

The muscle in her cheek spasmed. *Not so relaxed now, are you, Iris?*

"Do you think their relationship is relevant to her murder?" the High Priestess asked.

I shrugged. "Could be. It was a pretty big secret to carry around, especially since she was the Maiden. Major repercussions if anyone discovered the truth."

Iris lowered her gaze to the ground. "I knew about their relationship. It was difficult not to know. All you needed to do was stand in their presence for five minutes to feel the intense connection between them."

"Did you ever see anything firsthand?"

Iris shifted her gaze out to the ocean. I moved to stand beside her. It really was a gorgeous vista.

"Yes, one time. Fleur was meant to bring me herbs from the greenhouse for a ceremony we were preparing together. She was taking longer than usual, so I went to the greenhouse to see if I could help."

"And you saw her there with Uri?"

She nodded once. "It was a shock. They were kissing. I knew they loved each other and had for years, but I expected more discipline from Fleur. She knew how easily she could slip up, once hormones were hard at work."

I could relate. Marley was the direct result of my hardworking hormones.

"Did she see you?" I asked.

Iris shook her head. "I was glad of that. I don't know what she would have done had she realized."

"You must've been angry with her, even if you didn't tell her what you'd seen," I said.

Iris inhaled deeply and closed her eyes, allowing the

warmth of the sun to comfort her. "Not anger. Only disappointment."

"You wanted a Maiden who followed the rules," I said. It was more of a statement than a question.

She opened her eyes. "Of course. I'd invested so much time and energy in Fleur's training. What kind of High Priestess would I be if I treated our oaths so disrespectfully? I still feel guilty when I think of her."

My ears perked up. Guilt? Was this a confession?

"I understand that hemlock can be a peaceful way to die," I said. "Whoever killed her must have cared for her."

She cast a sidelong glance at me. "I've had much the same thought."

Not a confession then.

"Ianthe seems like a better choice for the Maiden," I said. "She's very dedicated."

Iris gave me a sad smile. "She is that."

"Did you choose Ianthe as Fleur's replacement?" I asked.

"It's never an individual choice," Iris said. "The coven leadership decides based on a set of criteria."

I was not getting positive vibes from her regarding Ianthe. I decided to dig a little deeper.

"Ianthe didn't seem to know the truth about Uri," I said.

"I'm not surprised," Iris said. "If she had, she would've used it to try to have Fleur removed from her position."

"Why didn't you?" I asked. "If you were concerned about Fleur's dedication, why didn't you have her removed?"

Iris sighed. "I had a soft spot for Fleur. I knew if she could get through this challenging phase, that she'd make an excellent High Priestess someday."

"You knew about her academic struggles, too, didn't you?"

"Yes," she admitted. "She confided in me about her need to rely on Garland and others for her excellent grades. She appreciated everyone's support. She was a grateful girl."

There was no way Iris killed Fleur. Quite the opposite. She'd overlooked all the girl's flaws because of her great affection for her.

"You could get in trouble with the coven for hiding this information, couldn't you?"

Iris nodded. "Stripping Fleur of her title was well within my power."

"Even though you only saw them kissing?" I queried.

"It would be sufficient to call her position into question," Iris said. "It was my duty to report what I knew, so that the coven could decide whether to call forth Fleur's replacement."

"But you didn't want Ianthe as your understudy, you wanted Fleur."

"I wanted Fleur," she confirmed. "It didn't matter to me what her shortcomings were. She'd proven herself to be a worthy Maiden all the same."

"And now you're stuck with Ianthe."

Iris placed her palms together, as if in prayer. "I love all members of the coven. Ianthe and I will do well together. Have no fear of that. But I will miss Fleur dearly." A single tear slid down her cheek.

I couldn't possibly rat out the High Priestess to the rest of the coven. For one thing, I'd make a powerful enemy. More importantly, though, I liked that she was willing to bend for someone she cared about. It was exactly what my aunt was trying to do for me now. Other than my father and Karl, I wasn't accustomed to having anyone in my corner. Her unfortunate death aside, Fleur was a lucky girl.

"Your secret is safe with me," I assured her. I wasn't the most affectionate person, but I found myself placing a comforting hand on her arm. "And I'm sorry for your loss, High Priestess."

She placed her hand over mine. "Please, call me Iris."

CHAPTER 17

AFTER THE EARLY morning interview of Iris, my body was begging for caffeine. It wasn't often that I was up at the butt crack of dawn, and I didn't intend to make a habit of it. I remembered Tanya mentioning a coffee shop near Willow Park called the Caffeinated Cauldron, so I decided to check it out.

The Caffeinated Cauldron was teeming with people when I arrived. It appeared to be the 'before work' crowd, getting their fix before a long day at the office or on the retail floor. I stepped up to the counter expecting to order something basic like a hazelnut coffee. My gaze traveled over the menu on the wall and I quickly realized this was no Starbucks. Everything seemed to have a magical bent. Based on the number of unfamiliar words, I'd need an interpreter to help me figure out what to order.

"You look confused," the barista said. "Is there something I can help you with?" She was a petite brunette with a sprinkle of freckles. Not small enough or green enough to be a leprechaun.

"I'm new here," I said. "I mean, *really* new here, and I have no idea what any of these descriptions mean. What's a lava latte?"

The barista smiled. "That one has a bit of a kick to it."

"A kick? As in a lot of caffeine?"

"There's caffeine in it, but it's magic that gives it the real flavor." She glanced up at the menu. "Tell me what experience you're looking for, and I'll see if I can point you to the right drink."

What experience was I looking for? I was in a coffee shop, not a theme park. I pondered the menu. "I'm looking to wake up and get through the rest of the day without crashing. I was up earlier than usual and I need to not crawl under my desk for a two-hour nap."

"Well, we have several options for you, in that case. We have the Bippity Bop latte, the Halo Effect latte, and you can get any coffee with a shot of these." She pointed to a long list on the left side of the menu.

"What's a shot of brain booster?" I asked. If that made me smarter, I was all over it.

"Clears the cobwebs from your mind," the barista said. "People tend to get that at the beginning or end of the day."

Made sense. "I'll try a black coffee with a shot of eyes-wide-open."

"Good choice." The barista moved swiftly to prepare my drink. Across the room, I spotted a familiar figure in a perfectly tailored light gray suit and a pale pink tie. He was seated at a table with another man I didn't know. The man had brown hair and a scruffy beard, but it was the two small horns on his head that caught my attention. Who was Mr. Hale having coffee with—the Jersey devil?

I paid for my coffee, took a long sip, and went to greet my boss. He'd want to know about my conversation with Iris.

I approached him from behind and clapped a hand on his broad shoulder.

"Fancy meeting you here, boss. I was desperate for some artificial energy. It isn't every day that I get up before the sun, although I guess you're used to that." My mouth seemed to be moving faster than normal and that was saying something.

"Good morning, Miss Rose," Mr. Hale said. He did not look pleased to see me. It occurred to me that this was not a social meeting. Then I remembered the story he mentioned at the soccer game.

I snapped my fingers. "Oh, this must be your source for the blood contamination story," I said. I turned and faced the horned man. "Dude, give him all the information you have. If someone is covering up a deadly mistake like that, they deserve to have their derriere nailed to the wall."

The man stiffened and glanced quickly at Mr. Hale. "Alec?"

I began to get a bad feeling about my word vomit.

"Miss Rose, allow me to introduce you to Craig Dean, the CEO of Bloodspring."

Popcorn balls.

I did my best to make light of it. "Of course I know this is Mr. Dean," I said. "You know how I love to say ridiculous things that have absolutely no basis in reality." I gave Mr. Dean a playful punch on the arm. "You don't know this about me, but I am a huge practical joker. Mr. Hale is learning the hard way."

Anger flashed in his blue eyes. "Yes, the hard way, indeed."

I had to get out of Dodge before he lost his temper. My gut told me that a restrained vampire like Alec Hale harbored the worst kind of temper.

"It was nice to meet you, Mr. Dean. I'll be in the office, Mr. Hale, writing up my notes from my talk with Iris."

I didn't wait for a response. I hightailed it out of the coffee shop and hustled back to the office, resisting the urge to look over my shoulder. If I could type up my story quickly, then I could escape before Mr. Hale returned. I was fairly certain this was the kind of mistake that would cost me my job.

Bentley and Tanya were in the office when I got there.

"What's wrong with you?" Bentley asked, tactful as usual. "You look like you've seen a ghost."

I stopped short. "Is that possible here?" Although I'd taken witches, werewolves, and vampires in stride, I wasn't so sure about ghosts.

"Not likely," he said. "Unless you're a psychic or a sorceress."

Not entirely comforting. It implied that there *were* ghosts afoot, but I just couldn't see them.

"I'd offer you a drink," Tanya said, "but I can see you already have a coffee. Did you happen to see Mr. Hale in there? I know he was meeting with Mr. Dean from Bloodspring."

"Yes," I said, dropping into my chair. "I discovered that by accident." Me and my big mouth. "I thought he was meeting with his source for the blood contamination story."

Bentley shot me a look of concern. "Technically, he was. He'd been meeting with Craig Dean under the pretense of talking about investing in a new community pool, but he was using it as an excuse to listen to his thoughts. That's how Alec learned of the incident in the first place. He caught a snippet of Mr. Dean's thoughts in a restaurant and decided to dig further."

I covered my face with my hands. And now I had completely blown his cover. Mr. Dean would be able to hide any evidence of wrongdoing and Mr. Hale wouldn't get his story.

I was doomed.

"What happened, Rose?" Bentley asked. "Why do I get the feeling that you said something you shouldn't have?"

I peeked at him through my fingers. "Because I always say something I shouldn't have. It's the highlight of my personality. Haven't you figured that out yet?"

Bentley sighed and rolled his chair closer to mine. "Listen, we all make mistakes. The fact that Alec hasn't come back to the office yet, ready to annihilate you, is a good sign, right? Maybe you didn't say as much as you think you did."

I repeated the conversation in Caffeinated Cauldron.

"Okay, forget everything I said," Bentley groaned. "You're ashes in a Phoenix's fire."

I didn't know what the expression meant, but it sounded like I was dead meat. "Is he going to fire me?"

Tonya and Bentley exchanged uneasy glances.

"He doesn't suffer fools gladly," Tanya said.

Well, that was something he and I had in common.

"Tell you what," Bentley said. "Why don't you write up whatever it is you came to do and leave it here? Then stay out of sight as long as possible and maybe it will blow over. I'll make sure he gets your work."

I stared at Bentley. "Why are you being nice to me? I thought you didn't want me here. Another legacy hire, remember?"

Bentley shrugged. "Purely for selfish reasons. It's kind of nice having someone lower than me in the ranks. As you can see, we're a barebones staff."

Selfish or not, I appreciated his support. "Okay, I'm going to whip this up as quickly as I can and then go into hiding. Possibly forever."

I opened the laptop on the desk and typed up my conversation with Iris. I wrote it the way I would have told the story to Mr. Hale in the office. Blunt and concise. I didn't have time to spruce it up and ponder Marley's list of fancy words.

"I've emailed you a copy," I told Bentley. "I don't want to

email him directly." Not like he could climb out of the screen and get me. He wasn't the freaky character in *The Ring*, after all.

"I'll pray for you," Tanya said.

"Thanks." I wasn't sure which deity she prayed to, but it didn't really matter. I needed all the help I could get.

I hid in the cottage until it was time to pick up Marley from school. There was still no word from Mr. Hale. I decided to have a look at the job listings in town to see what other options existed for me. I suspected there would not be much I was qualified to do and I was right. I could get a cashier job at one of the grocery stores, but the money would not be very much. Although we were currently living rent-free, I wasn't sure whether that was a permanent arrangement. What if I suddenly needed to cover greater expenses? How would I manage? Fear shot through me at the prospect of failing Marley once again. That little girl had had enough disappointment in her life. I couldn't be another speed bump on her life's highway. I was her mother; I was supposed to be giving her the best start in life.

After PP3 and I walked Marley home from school, I watched as she did her homework without complaint and without request for help. She was so self-sufficient, so unlike me. How did I manage to produce a child like this?

"Everything okay today, Mom?" she asked over dinner. I'd made homemade macaroni and cheese with the breadcrumb topping that she liked. Anything to alleviate my guilt.

"What makes you think something's wrong?"

"Because you're quiet," she said. "You're only quiet if there's a problem. That's your tell."

I managed a smile. "Oh, I have a tell, do I?"

"Did something happen at work?" she pressed on. "Or

with the murder investigation?"

I ruffled her hair. "No, everything's fine." I hesitated. "You've been doing so well here. You've been braver than I ever thought possible. I'm really proud of you."

Marley eyed me carefully. "If you're trying to get me to stop sleeping in your bed, it's not going to work. Yours is still more comfortable."

Although Marley had made great strides in the food department since our arrival, she was still my regular bedtime buddy. Baby steps.

"What would you say if I had Mrs. Babcock hang out with you tonight?"

Marley considered me for a moment. She must have sensed my need to get out of the cottage because she didn't object. "Sounds good to me. We can play chess again. She's pretty good."

"Great, I'll call her."

I had to put distance between us tonight, not because I didn't want to spend time with her, but because I felt like I didn't deserve to spend time with her. I didn't know where I would go. I just needed to think about how I could make things right, assuming that was even possible.

I left on foot once Mrs. Babcock arrived. I called each of my cousins to see if I could rustle up a drinking buddy, but no one was available. Linnea had guests at the inn to tend to, Aster was attending a board meeting, and Florian had a date with a smoking hot fairy. It was Florian who suggested I try The Wishing Well.

"I think you'll be comfortable there," Florian told me. "And it's not a vampire hangout. If you're hiding from Alec, he's unlikely to find you there."

I doubted I'd be comfortable anywhere in Starry Hollow right now, but I took his suggestion and headed over to the bar. Maybe The Wishing Well would live up to its name.

CHAPTER 18

I SAT IN THE BAR, nursing my drink and trying not to feel like a complete and utter failure. I knew I wasn't smart enough for this job. That I'd screw it up eventually. Family or not, Aunt Hyacinth couldn't possibly think I was a good addition to the staff after this. I'd made her look stupid for believing in me.

I pressed my palm against my forehead and sighed. I only hoped Marley wasn't too disappointed in me. It was her opinion that mattered most.

"What are you drinking?" the bartender asked.

I glanced up quickly, only to realize he wasn't speaking to me, which made sense, given that he was the one who'd made my drink in the first place.

"I'll have what she's having," a familiar voice said. I looked over to see Sheriff Nash sitting beside me. He wore jeans and a tight black T-shirt that showed off his muscular arms. Off-duty clothes.

"Are you sure about that, Sheriff?" the bartender asked. "She's having a rum and Coke."

The sheriff grimaced. "You know me too well, Bo. Pour some whiskey in there instead of rum and I'll be good to go."

"You got it." The bartender pulled down a bottle from the shelf to start the sheriff's drink.

"What's got you crying dragon tears, Rose?" the sheriff asked.

"Dragon tears? Is that a thing?"

He shrugged. "It's an expression in the paranormal world. I suspect you'll be hearing a lot of those from now on, so you may as well get used to them."

I took another sip of my drink. "It seems like there's so much for me to get used to. I'm not sure I can handle it."

He made a face of mock surprise. "I'm sorry. I'm pretty sure I just heard the Jersey girl say there was something she couldn't handle." He tapped his ear, as though trying to clear an obstruction. "I couldn't possibly have heard that correctly. Do you want to say it again?"

"You're hilarious," I said. "Are you sure that gold star you wear isn't in recognition of your comic genius?"

The bartender set the sheriff's drink in front of him.

"Put it on my tab, will you? And hers, too."

Bo nodded and moved to the other end of the bar where two more patrons had settled down on stools.

"So tell me, Rose. What is it you can't handle? I'd like to know."

I turned away from him and stared into the darkness of my drink. "You wouldn't understand."

"What is it that you think I wouldn't understand? Feeling like a unicorn out of the meadow?"

I scrunched my nose. "Another paranormal expression? Do you know any human ones?"

He rubbed his chin thoughtfully. "Fish out of water?"

I nodded. "That'll do." I polished off my drink in one large swallow. "I've tried so hard to do what's best for Marley. And now we find ourselves with a chance to start over and do better, but I'm still messing up. I'm being given opportunities that I don't deserve, and I still can't seem to make it work. The only thing I've shown my daughter is how to fail at life." I didn't know why I was confiding in him. I blamed the alcohol.

"What happened? Wait, let me guess. You upset your vampire boss."

"You might say that." I wasn't about to get into the details. The sheriff already thought I was an idiot. No need to give him evidence.

"Newsflash, Rose. Alec Hale thinks everyone who isn't him is a moron. It doesn't make it true."

"Do you two have a history or something? You really don't seem to like each other very much."

Before he could answer, Bo placed another rum and Coke on the bar in front of me. Now that was what I called service.

"I told you before," Sheriff Nash said. "It's the natural order of things. Werewolves and vampires tend to be at odds."

Despite his reasoning, I still got the feeling there was more to the story than he was telling me.

"So why are you here?" I asked.

He finished his drink in one long, slow gulp. "This is my regular watering hole. I tend to come here after work to relax." He paused. "Naturally, that got shot to minotaur shit tonight when I walked in and saw you."

Instinctively, I reached out and smacked his leg. "Hey, that's rude."

He laughed at my unexpected and violent reaction. "You're lucky I'm off duty or I'd arrest you right now."

"On what charge? It was self-defense."

He grinned and I noticed the attractive way his dark eyes crinkled at the corners.

"I'd charge you with abusing the sheriff," he replied.

"That's not a real offense," I said.

"It's offensive to me," he said quickly. He raised his finger and Bo was there in a heartbeat with another drink. "You're the best, Bo."

"Why do you come alone?" I asked. "There's no Mrs. Sheriff to help you relax at home?"

His expression darkened. "No, I can't say there is." Again, I felt like there was a story there, but I didn't push the issue. If there was one thing I'd learned today, it was that I needed to keep my big mouth shut more often.

"How's the investigation going?" I asked. Although I realized it was slightly dangerous ground, I wanted to change the subject. "Are you sure you didn't follow me here because you still think I'm a suspect?"

"I'm working on a theory," he said. "You'll be happy to know it doesn't involve you."

"Well, that's a relief," I said. "I can cross one reason off the My Life Is In The Toilet list."

He grinned again. "Glad I could be of service."

"So how much do you hate my family?" I asked. "On a scale of one to a million?"

"I don't have the energy for hate," he said. "I just wish they weren't so damned entitled all the time. I mean, I'm a werewolf. I could give two hoots about the One True Witch."

"But what if it was the One True Werewolf? Which would still be 'OTW,' by the way. Wouldn't you think that was pretty special?"

The sheriff tipped back his glass. "Maybe," he said. "I never really gave it much thought. Who knows? Maybe I am the descendent of the very first werewolf. Although, technically, wouldn't all werewolves be descendants of the original werewolf?"

I gave him a sly look. "Same might even be said for witches."

He snorted in that charming way he seemed to have. "I wouldn't be bringing that common sense to the dinner table at Thornhold," he advised. "You don't want to risk getting on your aunt's bad side. Trust me, I know."

"It seems to me it's more your brother who gets under her skin."

"Yeah, my brother tends to be more ass than wolf. Still, he's my brother and I'll defend him with my last breath."

"I really like Linnea," I said. "It's a shame they couldn't make their marriage work."

"Me, too," the sheriff said.

I tapped my fingernails on the side of my glass. "Do you think if Linnea had been a werewolf or your brother had been a wizard that their relationship would have lasted? Maybe the whole Romeo and Juliet thing was too much for them."

"Hard to say," he replied. "If Wyatt weren't a werewolf, it's likely his whole personality would be different. He's very wolf-like as far as werewolves go, hence the womanizing." He paused, thinking. "Anyway, it doesn't matter. It's not like he could become a wizard or she could become a werewolf. That only works with…"

The realization hit us at the same time.

"Vampires," we said in unison, and looked at each other in surprise.

"Sweet baby Elvis, I know what happened to Fleur."

"You know about Uri?" he asked. "I thought I told you to stay out of my investigation."

"How did you find out?" I asked.

He ignored my question. "Do you really think…?"

"I don't think. I know." I remembered something Delphine

Winter had said when Marley and I were at the library. "Can you get us into the high school after hours?"

He burped. "Of course I can. I'm the sheriff, remember?"

"You're also drunk."

"Not enough to count. Takes a lot of liquor to bring down a werewolf."

I eyed him. "Should we call your deputy?"

He shook his head. "He'll be fast asleep at this hour. Let's just go to the school. That's easy enough to do without causing any trouble." He looked at me askance. "Although I probably shouldn't say that when I'm sitting this close to you."

I smacked his leg again. "Hey," I objected. "I haven't been the root of any trouble here." Yet.

He threw money on the bar and hopped off the stool. "Let's go before I come to my senses."

CHAPTER 19

THE HIGH SCHOOL was eerily dark and quiet. Not a surprise given the late hour.

In the corridor, Sheriff Nash strode a few steps ahead of me and I wondered whether that was an alpha male thing. Usually I was the fast walker in a group. I had to admit, it wasn't a bad view from the back. Those jeans fit him like a denim glove. It was easy to see why women wanted him and men wanted to be him. The swagger alone was worth a five-minute ogle.

He stopped walking and waited for me to catch up. "You've got a dreamy expression right now," he said. "Where'd you go? Back to New Jersey for a slice of pizza?"

"No," I said, snapping to attention. No way did I want him to know what I'd been thinking. He would love that a little too much. Or maybe he wouldn't. I wasn't sure which would bother me more.

"The janitor said Uri's locker is number 117."

"Do you have everyone in town's number on speed dial?" I asked.

"I'm the sheriff," he said. "I know a lot of people here. Comes with the job."

We found Uri's locker and the sheriff easily popped open the door. I pulled the contents from the shelf, including a stale sandwich and multiple empty folders.

"He's not a neat freak, is he?" I asked.

"He's a teenaged vampire," Sheriff Nash said. "What do you expect?"

"I don't know. Mr. Hale is so…fastidious."

Sheriff Nash widened his eyes. "Now there's a fancy word. Will you be using fastidious in any forthcoming articles, perchance?"

I moved to smack him again, but he anticipated me this time and dodged my hand.

"Has anyone ever told you that you have a violent streak?" he asked, grinning.

"That's just Jersey affection," I said.

"I'd hate to see you in love," he said, and then quickly seemed to think better of it. He cleared his throat. "So what are we looking for?"

"A book." I spotted it tucked under a crumpled Starry Hollow sweatshirt.

"*Vampire Transitions*," the sheriff read aloud. His expression hardened. "This is a solid piece of evidence, Rose. Good job."

I handed him the book. "You should probably keep hold of this until tomorrow."

"Tomorrow?" the sheriff repeated. "I'm calling Uri down to the station now. I'll even pick him up if I have to. This is a murder investigation. If Uri is responsible, he doesn't deserve one more peaceful night's sleep."

I wasn't convinced it was as cut and dry as that.

He pulled out his phone and dialed. "You should go home and get some rest. You've got a job to save tomorrow."

I watched as the sheriff headed down the corridor, clutching the book under his arm. Yep, that swagger was irritatingly alluring.

I turned back to the locker and took my time replacing the contents I'd removed. Why rush back to the cottage when Marley was asleep by now anyway?

I walked down the corridor and pretended that I was in *The Breakfast Club*, trapped in school after hours. I'd loved that movie as a teenager. My father had introduced me to the movies of John Hughes and they still held a special place in my heart. I remembered that he'd once said there was all kinds of magic in the world and that movies were one of them. It hadn't occurred to me then that he'd included literal magic in that statement. I had so many questions for him now that I knew the truth. Questions I'd never be able to ask him. I wondered what he would think if he could see me now.

A sound at the far end of the corridor grabbed my attention.

"Sheriff Nash?" I called. Or maybe it was the janitor coming to check on things.

"What are you doing here?" a voice asked.

I jerked around to see Uri. "I should ask you the same thing. Didn't the sheriff ask you to come to the station?"

"I stopped here to pick something up first," he said, eyeing me suspiciously.

"If you mean the book, you're too late," I said. "Sheriff Nash has it."

Panic streaked across Uri's features.

"You're already a vampire, Uri," I said. "Why would you need a book on transitioning to become one?"

"It was for a class assignment," he stuttered. He was a far cry from the smooth stylings of Alec Hale.

I sighed softly. "You're not a very good liar, Uri. I'm

surprised you managed to hide your relationship with Fleur for as long as you did." His fangs popped out and I jumped back a step. "Whoa. Are you threatening me? Because that is *not* a good idea."

His fangs retracted and his brow creased. "I...I don't know."

Fangs or not, I was pretty sure I could take him—unless he had crazy vampire strength. I really needed A Beginner's Guide To Crazy Crap I Didn't Know Existed.

"You don't want to hurt anyone else, Uri," I said. "I can tell you feel awful about what happened to Fleur."

He blinked. "Hurt anyone else?" He slapped his hands over his face. "You don't understand. *I* didn't poison Fleur. She took the hemlock herself."

A wave of understanding crashed over me. Of course she did. Now it all made sense. My emotions shifted between sympathy and anger.

"I know what happened, Uri," I said, as softly as a New Jersey woman could manage—my tone landed somewhere between a DMV employee and a Real Housewife at a drunken dinner party.

He fanned the fingers that were covering his face and peered at me through the gaps. "You do?"

"I think so. Should I run it past you?"

"Yeah." He slid down the wall to sit on the floor.

Instead of continuing to tower over him, I moved to sit beside him. There was no need to intimidate him, not now.

"You loved her very much, didn't you?" I tried my best to rub the hard edges from my tone.

Tears began streaming down his cheeks. "Of course I did. She was the blood in my veins."

I wondered whether he meant literally or figuratively. It was hard to know with a vampire.

"I wanted us to be together for eternity."

"And she wanted that, too?" I queried.

He nodded emphatically. "It was her idea to become a vampire. She knew how much Iris cared about her, so she figured the only way out of being the Maiden was to stop being a witch and become a vampire. Then we'd be free to follow our own path."

"Did you know that Iris saw you together in the greenhouse?" I asked.

Uri nodded. "That's when Fleur made the decision. She knew that if violating the Maiden pact wasn't enough to disqualify her, she'd need to do something more extreme."

"Was she conflicted about it at all?" I asked. "Did she hate being a witch that much?"

He sniffed. "She didn't hate being a witch at all, but she never wanted to be the Maiden. She felt obligated because it's such a big honor. Really, she wanted us to be together more than anything." He sighed. "And I wanted that, too."

"You didn't seek help from anyone with transition experience?"

"It's illegal except in special cases. She was sure that we could manage the transformation together. She stole the book from the library and we studied it from cover to cover. Fleur had so much left to give." His voice cracked.

That much was true. Whatever her flaws, the Maiden was a witch with a bright future. But no more. Love had a way of wrecking the most solid plans. I knew that all too well. Although I wouldn't trade Marley for anything in the world, in a way, the birth of a new life signaled the death of my old one.

"Did you steal the hemlock for her?" I asked.

"No, she took it from coven headquarters when she and Iris were there to prepare for a ceremony. She got everything herself, except the vampire blood she needed. I gave that to her. We agreed to meet in the woods, where no one would accidentally find us. She wanted me there when she woke up." His shoulders began to shake as his crying intensified. "But she never did. We never should have tried to do it on our own."

Or at all. But I didn't want to argue with him in his current state.

"Uri, why didn't you just tell everyone this when it first happened? You could've saved people a lot of grief."

"Because I knew that it would be my fault," he said. "They can't blame her because she's dead, so the witches would come after me. After all, I'm the wayward vampire that corrupted their beloved Maiden. Wouldn't you want to prosecute me?"

He made a good point. The coven was definitely inclined to blame him under the circumstances. She'd been the perfect embodiment of a young Silver Moon coven witch until Uri caught her innocent eye. And now she was dead.

"What about Victorine Del Bianco?" I asked. "Will the vampire coven support you?"

Uri wiped away his tears. "I don't know. I guess I'll have to ask now that my secret is out." He cast a sidelong glance at me. "How did you figure it out?"

"When I stopped using my head, and started using…other parts of my body," I replied. "After that, it was obvious."

He gazed at me with a mixture of disappointment and admiration. "You really are a Rose, aren't you?"

I had no idea what that meant, but I decided to take it as a compliment.

"I suppose I am."

The sound of skidding footsteps caught us off guard. Uri and I glanced up to see Sheriff Nash racing toward us.

"Rose, are you hurt?" he asked, sliding across the floor on his knees to get to us faster.

Uri and I exchanged bemused glances.

"Do I look hurt?" I asked.

The sheriff blinked. "No." He noticed Uri's tears. "You're crying." He shot me an accusatory look. "What did you do to him?"

I gave an exasperated huff. "One second you're worried that he's attacked me and now you're worried I've attacked him?" I narrowed my eyes. "Make up your mind, Sheriff."

"I don't know, Rose. You've confused me."

"We're having a little talk," I said. "Uri has some important information for you and it isn't necessarily what you think." I helped Uri to his feet. "You don't need to be afraid of the Big Bad Wolf, Uri. Tell the sheriff what really happened. Fleur wouldn't want you to be held responsible for this."

Sheriff Nash's gaze shifted from me to Uri. "Miss Rose is right. Let us help you."

Uri nodded and proceeded to tell the sheriff everything.

CHAPTER 20

MR. HALE'S melodic voice cut through the quiet of the office. "Miss Rose, I'm surprised to see you here."

I hadn't even heard him approach my desk. For a vampire, he moved like a ghost. Or a predator. Hmm. Let's go with ghost. A ghost was less likely to rip out my vocal chords with fangs.

"Now that Fleur's death has been solved, I was finishing my article. I figured I owed you that much before you kicked me to the curb."

"It's a rather poetic story, isn't it?" Mr. Hale said. "Risking one's life in the name of love."

"A young girl died before she had a chance to really live," I said. "I'd hardly call that poetic. In my experience, it's never smart to change who you are for anyone."

He surprised me by taking the empty seat beside me. Was he trying to get close to check my veins for potency? I wondered what his position was on varicose veins. To the human eye, they were highly unattractive, but maybe they were a hot commodity in a vampire's world.

"You're not much of a romantic, are you?" he asked.

ANNABEL CHASE

"I haven't seen much in the world to suggest I should be."

He adjusted his cufflinks. "You're still so young and much of the world has been closed to you until now."

"What? You mean Starry Hollow and magic?"

He gave a crisp nod. "I would think you'd find it all rather enchanting."

"It's been an eye-opener, that's for sure. Maybe if I were some dreamy-eyed Podunk from Knights-in-Shining-Armor Town, I'd feel more...enchanted."

His sensual mouth formed a thin line. "Knights-in-Shining-Armor Town? Isn't that adjacent to Happily-Ever-Afterville?"

My brow lifted. "A sense of humor, Mr. Hale? And here I thought the centuries of immortal angst had eroded it from your system."

"So you do know big words," he said. "Perhaps try using one or two of them in your writing next time."

My ears perked up. "Next time?"

He gave me an amused look. "Unless you were planning to seek other employment."

"You're not firing me?" I pressed my lips together. "Is this because of my aunt...?"

He waved me off. "Not at all. Yes, you made an egregious error and I was...less than pleased with you. However, you've shown yourself to possess many of the qualities we look for in a journalist. You've proven yourself to be tenacious, resourceful, and—dare I say it—intelligent."

I straightened in my chair. Wow. High praise, indeed. "Thanks. I don't think I've heard that many complimentary adjectives since I walked by the construction site on Ferry Avenue at lunchtime."

He allowed himself a small smile. "You're so unlike the rest of your family."

"And you're surprised because...? I didn't grow up with a Silver Moon spoon in my mouth, remember?"

"And you have your mother's coloring, as well as her attitude," he said softly. "I'm sure that ruffles the end of your aunt's broomstick."

Wait. What? "You knew my mother?"

His green eyes widened slightly. "Of course. Why wouldn't I have?"

"It...It just never occurred to me. You're a turned vampire, right? Not like Uri."

He sniffed. "Yes, turned, of course."

Ah, a pecking order even among vampires.

"How old are you exactly?" I asked.

"A gentlemanly vampire never reveals his true age."

"Really? I thought vampires were all about throwing their ages around. Like measuring their..."

He cleared his throat. "As I said, a *gentlemanly* vampire..."

Right. "So you knew my mother."

"Mmm."

"Were you two ever an item?" *Please say no. Please say no.*

"No."

Phew.

"She and your father were destined for each other," he said. "It was clear to everyone who knew them." He gave me a wry smile. "So it's interesting to me that two romantics like your parents could produce...you."

"Well, in case it's escaped your memory, one of my parents died when I was a baby and the other one was left to raise me alone, so not sure that the destined-for-each-other thing worked out in the end."

He studied me for a moment—so closely that I felt his breath warm on my neck. My pulse picked up the pace and I hoped like hell his vampire hearing didn't detect the rapid beat of my heart.

Finally, he clucked his tongue. "So cynical, Ember Rose. Perhaps Starry Hollow will cure what ails you."

I bristled. "Nothing *ails* me, thank you very much."

He met my firm gaze. "Apologies. Offending you was not my intent."

"That's quite all right, Alec," I said, and caught the flicker of surprise in his eyes. No more Mr. Hale. From now on, he was Alec to me and he was going to like it.

"I've written a story on Fleur, as well," he said. "I took it over from Bentley."

"Why? I thought you assigned it to me."

"And I wasn't certain what the outcome would be." He placed the papers on the desk in front of me. "Would you like to read it and decide which one is best to use? No pressure to use mine, of course."

Now it was my turn to show surprise. "Me? Why would I know which one is best? You're the big deal editor."

"Isn't it obvious? You have gotten to know Fleur better than anyone in this office. You asked the right questions and elicited the right answers from your interview subjects." He placed a strong hand on my arm and the effect was nothing short of electric. "I think you might make a fine journalist one day, given the proper training."

"I think so, too," I said, trying my best to sound confident.

"Not to mention your continued employment here will exacerbate the sheriff's persistent foul mood," he added with a mischievous grin.

"You two really dislike each other, don't you?"

He gave a modest shrug. "Werewolves and vampires have never been the best of friends under any circumstances."

"Well, you're in good company because he doesn't seem to care for my family very much either."

"I know, which is why it pleases me to no end that you're a Rose." He rolled back the chair and stood. "Have a pleasant evening, Miss Rose. I expect I'll see you bright and early tomorrow."

"Goodnight...Alec."

It was only after he left the office that his statement dawned on me. Why on earth did it please him that the sheriff didn't care for me? I had no idea. Too bad I couldn't read *his* mind.

I lifted the papers from my desk and began to read.

Prescott Peabody III ran to the front door, barking like a crazy dog.

"What's the matter, buddy?" I asked. No one knocked or rang the bell. Maybe Florian was out in the field shooting birds or taking down broomsticks, although I didn't hear any gunshots.

I opened the front door and peered outside. Nothing and no one. As I went to close the door, my gaze dropped to the front step and I saw the potted flower.

"Oh." I lifted the white ceramic pot and admired the single purple flower. I recognized it as an orchid like the ones Garland had shown me in the high school greenhouse.

Marley joined me in the doorway. "How pretty. Is there a card?"

I turned the pot from side to side. "No card." I brought it into the house and closed the door. "Where should I put it?"

"I think orchids need lots of sunlight. I'll look it up." Marley retrieved her tablet from the coffee table.

"Maybe I should leave it in your capable hands," I told her. "You know I kill all living things."

Marley smiled. "That's not true. You've done a pretty good job with PP3 and me."

"Yes, but you're easy," I said, rubbing the top of her head. "I just water you and feed you and you seem to thrive." It was nothing to do with me. Marley was a marvel all on her own.

"You don't give yourself enough credit, Mom," Marley said. "Yes, it says here to put it somewhere with lots of light."

I placed the pot on the ledge of the kitchen counter, above the sink but below the decorative willow heart.

"It looks nice there," Marley said. "Just don't forget to water it."

"You'll need to send me daily email reminders," I said.

"You're not *that* forgetful," Marley replied. "Who do you think left it for you?"

I honestly had no idea. Garland and I had talked about flowers, but it seemed unlikely that the herbology expert would anonymously drop off an orchid.

"We'll need to ask Aunt Hyacinth if her security cameras picked up anything," I said.

"Don't do that," Marley said. "Whoever left it obviously doesn't want you to know it was him."

I cocked an eyebrow. "And what makes you think it's a *him?*"

Marley giggled, reminding me of the ten-year-old that still lurked within the old soul of my daughter. "You're an eligible maiden in a village of knights. Of course it's a him."

"First of all, we've already established that I am definitely *not* a maiden, nor a damsel-in-distress. I don't need a knight because I don't need rescuing."

"Okay, fine. You don't *need* one, but does that mean you can't want one?"

I tousled her hair. "Right now, I'm perfectly content with PP3 and you."

She bonked me on the nose. "*Right now* is the important phrase in that sentence."

"Mind your own business, young lady. I don't need you taking an interest in my love life."

"Someone has to, if you expect to ever have one."

I dusted off my hands. "I don't expect to ever have one, so that solves that problem."

Marley groaned in exasperation. "Mom, this is our chance for a fresh start. You know Dad wouldn't want you to live the rest of your life alone. You're too young for that."

I kissed her forehead. "I'm not alone, silly."

"I'm already ten," she said. "In seven more years, I'll leave for college. You need to focus on yourself."

I popped my hands over my ears. "I can't hear you. La la la."

She rolled her eyes. "Very mature. Fine. Ignore the orchid. Ignore the town full of new opportunities."

I heaved a sigh. "I'm not ignoring anything, Marley. I'm just…not ready."

"Well, if you don't start making an effort soon," she warned, "I'm going to sign you up for every dating site in town. You won't be able to keep up."

My eyes bulged. "Do that and you won't see the outside of these four walls for the next seven years. Consider it your princess tower."

A knock on the front door startled us. I gave PP3 a sharp look. "Now you *don't* bark?"

Florian stood on the front step. "Mother asks that you come to dinner tonight in the main house. Word has gotten back to her and she wants to hear all about your recent adventures."

Oh, boy.

I fixed him with my hard stare. "Tell me the truth, Florian. Am I in trouble?"

He appeared surprised by the question. "In trouble? Goodness, no. Mother hasn't sounded this excited since she enrolled Precious in feline finishing school. Oh, and she also has your passports."

Our passports? "Then we accept the invitation." I called over my shoulder to Marley. "Come on, kid. We're wanted in the main house."

For a brief moment, I pondered those words. *We're wanted.*

"I'm right here," Marley said, standing beside me.

I took my daughter by the hand and followed Florian back to the family home.

If you want to find out about new releases by Annabel Chase, sign up for my newsletter here: http://eepurl.com/ctYNzf

Starry Hollow Witches

Magic & Murder, Book 1

Magic & Mystery, Book 2

Magic & Mischief, Book 3

Magic & Mayhem, Book 4

Magic & Mercy, Book 5

Magic & Madness, Book 6

Spellbound

Curse the Day, Book 1

Doom and Broom, Book 2

Spell's Bells, Book 3

Lucky Charm, Book 4

Better Than Hex, Book 5

Cast Away, Book 6

A Touch of Magic, Book 7

A Drop in the Potion, Book 8

Hemlocked and Loaded, Book 9

All Spell Breaks Loose, Book 10

Made in the USA
San Bernardino, CA
29 November 2018